A Death in
Cactus City

ALSO BY PATRICIA K. BATTA

A KATIE IN CACTUS MYSTERY

Book #1

A Death in Cactus City

PATRICIA K. BATTA

LILLIMAR PUBLISHING

PUBLISHED BY LILLIMAR PUBLISHING

www.lillimarpublishing.com

Cataloguing-in-Publication Data
Names: Batta, Patricia K., author.
Title: A death in Cactus City: a Katie in Cactus mystery / Patricia K. Batta.
Description: First edition. | Prescott, AZ : Lillimar Publishing, [2017] | Series:
A Katie in Cactus mystery ; book #1.
Identifiers: ISBN: 9781974638420 | LCCN: 2017912908
Subjects: LCSH: Lawyers—Fiction. | Arizona—Fiction. | Grandmothers—
Fiction. | Murder—Investigation—Fiction. | Detective and mystery
stories. | GSAFD: Mystery fiction. | LCGFT: Detective and mys-
tery fiction. | BISAC: FICTION / Mystery & Detective / Women
Sleuths.
Classification: LCC: PS3602.A898 D43 2017 | DDC: 813.54—dc23

This is a work of fiction. Don't look for Cactus City or a city like it in Arizona.
It isn't there. Definitely don't try to find a parallel with the Cactus City Police
Department. Thank goodness, that isn't there, either. With a few mountains
borrowed from here, some switchbacks from there, Cactus City is a completely
fictitious city set somewhere in Yavapai County, in an indeterminant area a reasonable distance from several locations you will be able to find. None of the characters
in this book are based on any persons, living or dead. Names, characters, places,
events, and incidents are either the product of the author's imagination or are used
fictitiously.

Cover photo copyright: <a href='https://www.123rf.com/profile_phartisan'>
phartisan / 123RF Stock Photo</a>

Cover and text design by Mary Jo Zazueta
www.tothepointsolutions.com

Printed in the United States of America
First Edition

A Death in
Cactus City

CHAPTER ONE

A loud pounding on the door propelled Kate to her feet.

"Help me! Please, help me!"

The shrill voice sent Kate stumbling through the dark unfamiliar room to the window. Pulling aside the edge of the curtain, she saw a willowy blonde, her light-blue eyes wide with alarm. Tears streamed down her face. Panic seemed to reach through the narrow opening. Kate didn't have time to worry about where she was or how she got here. This woman needed help, now.

When Kate threw the door open, a gush of cool air cleared her brain. She remembered. She had checked into this small motel at the edge of Cactus City, Arizona, that afternoon.

The woman grabbed Kate by the arm and pulled her outside to the room next door. "I called 911," she managed between sobs. "I don't know if they'll get here soon enough. I don't know how to help him."

Kate peered into a room eerily like her own. The sight of a tall man lying on his back across the earth-toned Navajo blanket on the bed brought her fully awake. He didn't appear to be breathing. Her feet didn't want to move, but she forced herself forward, her nose twitching at the rank odor. She couldn't see any vomit, so he must have made it to the bathroom, but his shirt was spattered with something. Could she remember enough CPR to try to revive him? Did she want to touch him?

Before she reached the bed, a man and a woman with EMT insignia on their shirts burst in and gently pushed her aside. She moved willingly, weak with relief that she didn't have to make contact.

"We'll take it from here," the man said. "It would be best if you left the room."

Kate backed out onto the walkway that ran in front of the motel rooms, pulling the woman with her. "That was fast," she said. "I didn't even hear the sirens. Did you?" But she realized she had heard them. She'd just been too stunned for them to register.

The woman looked bewildered, but at least the question made her stop shaking when she looked at Kate. "Were there sirens?"

While the male EMT checked the man over and began compressions on his chest, his female partner left and returned with a gurney. Kate and the distraught woman moved away from the door to give them room to work.

"What happened?" Kate asked, rubbing her arms. She couldn't tell if the chill was from the late-after-noon mountain air or the shock of what she had seen. She had fallen asleep fully clothed, but she was dressed for driving across the desert, not for the mile-and-a-bit-high mountains.

The woman was similarly dressed. Kate guessed she was a few years younger than her own age of thirty-five, probably in her mid-twenties. She was at least six inches taller than Kate's five feet five inches. Unbelievably long, tanned legs were topped by cutoff denim shorts and a lacy white blouse. She twisted the ends of a loose braid that hung over one shoulder, making Kate run her fingers through her own short, unruly, brunette curls.

"I don't know." The girl stopped, cocked her head, and frowned slightly. "We're on our way to Phoenix, to see Phil's father. We stopped for the night so we could get there early tomorrow. We went over to that little place for dinner." She pointed to a small building across the road with the name ZigZag Café embla-zoned in large green letters in the window. Putting her hand to her mouth, as if suppressing a sob, she closed her eyes for a moment. "Phil started feeling funny after we finished our salads, so we skipped the rest of dinner and came back to the room." Her brow was knit in concentration. Kate thought she was prob-ably trying to relate exactly what happened in order to make herself believe it. "He almost didn't make it to the bathroom before he got sick. He collapsed on the bed, but he looked so miserable. I thought it must be food poisoning and called 911. He started going into convulsions before I even hung up, so I ran out to try and find someone who could help. I don't know what I was thinking."

The EMTs rose from the man's side. The man pulled out a radio, punched one button, and spoke into it. Almost before Kate could process the fact that the EMTs had completely stopped working on the man, two uniformed policemen drove up in a squad car with "Cactus City Police" printed on its side. Kate felt a shiver of fear. Why were they here? Gathering their equipment, the EMTs shook their heads at the police officers and stepped away from the bed.

"What are they doing?" the woman cried. "Why did they stop?"

The younger of the officers, who looked hardly old enough to have graduated from high school, turned to them. "Who are you?" he asked.

"I'm Tiffany Wells," was the shrill reply. "That is my husband, Phil."

The officer put out a hand as if to steady her. "I'm sorry, but there was nothing the EMTs could do. Your husband is dead."

Kate barely had time to get her arms around Tiffany. Her knees almost gave under the weight of the taller woman.

"Do they know what happened?" Kate asked, struggling to keep Tiffany upright.

"No. That'll have to wait for the autopsy."

Tiffany shuddered.

"Do you have to do that?" Kate asked.

"Probably. The medical examiner will decide, but it is nearly always done in the case of sudden or unexplained death, and this appears to be both. Does he have any medical conditions that might have caused it?"

Tiffany's voice was filled with disbelief when she answered. "No. He is ... was healthy, worked out every day."

"All right. Someone will need to talk with you in a few minutes. Is there somewhere nearby you can wait?"

"She can come over here," Kate said and took Tiffany next door to her room, wrapped her in a Navajo blanket a bit too similar to the one on the bed next door, and deposited her in the one worn but comfortable-looking chair. She pulled a bottle of Jack Daniels out of her overnight bag and stared at it, wondering if it was the best thing to do. But, she could hardly have a drink herself without sharing. She retrieved two plastic glasses from the ice bucket tray and poured a little bourbon into each of them.

The woman took the glass without comment, sipped, took a larger drink, and closed her eyes. "Thank you," she managed after a moment. "I needed that."

"My name is Kate Christensen." Kate looked more closely at the woman. She had a smooth, even tan and a light touch of artfully applied makeup, now smeared by tears. *California*. Kate took a gulp of her own drink and added more bourbon to both glasses.

"I'm Tiffany Wells, but everyone calls me Tiff." The

woman glanced out the open doorway when another car pulled into the parking lot. A man emerged with a medical bag. "My husband's name is ..." She choked back a sob. "Was ... Phil." She took another drink before continuing. "We live in San Diego."

Aha, she was right. California girl. Kate smiled what she hoped was a comforting smile. "I arrived from Seattle this afternoon, but I might decide to stay in Cactus City."

Tiff stopped shaking and stared at Kate. "Really? Why would you move to this little place from a great city like that?"

Memories of the last few months came flooding back, but Kate wasn't ready to deal with them yet. She latched onto the most positive aspect of her move. "My grandmother lives here. She is becoming more fragile as she ages, but so far has insisted on staying in her own home. I thought it would be good for her to have some family close by to keep an eye on her. I expect to be here as long as she lives."

Tiff nodded. "I know, right? Phil's father recently married his caretaker. We're sure that was a big mistake, and we were hoping we could convince Dad to ditch her and come back to San Diego with us. Now ...." Her eyes filled with tears again. "Now I don't know what I'll do. I love Dad, but I'm not sure I can handle the responsibility by myself, even if I can convince him to leave the gold digger."

Kate glanced outside. Another car pulled into the parking lot. The ambulance was still there, along with the police cruiser and the medical examiner's car. Kate

6

frowned. Why was the ambulance still here? Weren't they supposed to be taking the body somewhere for an autopsy?

Kate poured another slug of bourbon into both glasses. Be careful, Kate, she thought. This woman could be an alcoholic for all you know. For now, the best way she could think of to help Tiff through this was to ply her with enough alcohol to deaden the pain.

Half an hour later, when the medical examiner was gone and the body was finally taken away, the young police officer came into the room. "The chief is finishing up now. He'll want to take statements from each of you, separately." He looked around and frowned as if wondering how to manage that.

Kate shook her head. "Excuse me? Why are the police involved?"

"A sudden, unexplained death always requires the police to investigate," he said. "We were alerted by the 911 call, the same as the EMTs, and they informed us when they determined the man was dead. Uh, maybe we should do this down at the station. We can't use the other room. We'd be contaminating a ..." He stopped and looked uncomfortable.

Kate stared at him. Really? Was he going to say crime scene?

"You can use this room to question both of us," Kate said. "I'll wait outside or in the motel lobby while you question Tiff. She has had quite a shock, so if you have to do this tonight, I hope you can do it here rather than drag her down to the police station."

The officer looked relieved. "Good idea." He retreated to make the arrangements.

"Thank you," Tiff said, her voice faint. "I don't know how I could handle the police station tonight." She looked at the bottle on the table beside Kate. "Could you top me off one more time before he comes to grill me?"

Kate thought if she were being grilled by the police she might want to keep her wits about her, but she couldn't make the decision for Tiff. She topped off Tiff's glass and her own as well. She paused with her glass halfway to her lips before remembering they planned to grill her after they finished with Tiff.

A few minutes later, a stocky man strutted into the room. "Police Chief Browning," he said, puffing out his chest. A glare from the chief told Kate it was time to leave. She grabbed her glass and a sweatshirt on her way out the door.

Halfway to the office, she stopped at a weathered picnic table and put down her glass to pull on the sweatshirt. She decided to stay outside and gaze at the distant mountain peaks silhouetted in the moon's glow. They were full of sharp angles, so different from the soft greens of the distant Olympic Mountains and expansive view of Puget Sound she had from her Seattle high-rise apartment. She wondered if she could turn her life around as drastically as her environment. She had left the high-speed life of a successful, stressed-out corporate attorney for several reasons, but she didn't know if she could find satisfaction in small-town life.

Waiting for her turn to be interrogated, she began to get nervous. She was sure they didn't always do this in cases of sudden death, at least not immediately. They must suspect something more than food poisoning. Had the officer really been about to say they would contaminate a crime scene? If so, Tiff was sure to be the main suspect. What had Kate let herself in for?

CHAPTER TWO

Even the sweatshirt couldn't make Kate feel comfortable as she sipped her bourbon while watching the young police officer search Tiff's car. Did they have a right to do that? When he finished, he went into Kate's room for a moment before walking out with the other officer who had arrived with him. They got into the squad car.

Kate's stomach rumbled with hunger. She could only hope to find somewhere to eat when they were finished with her. She eyed the café across the street as the two police officers entered it.

The police chief ambled out of her room. "Chief Browning," the stout, balding man announced as if she had already forgotten his name.

"Kate Christensen," she shot back, grabbing his proffered hand for a firm shake.

He blinked, which gave Kate a sliver of satisfaction. Several men had learned over the negotiating table that they wouldn't get anywhere trying to bully her.

"What brings you to Cactus City?" He pulled a half-smoked cigar out of his shirt pocket and lit it.

That must be why he decided to interrogate her outside. She resented being subjected to the cigar smoke, but resisted the urge to rub her arms and shiver to disrupt his plans. Instead, she folded her hands primly in front of her and gazed at him. The chief narrowed his eyes, as if he suspected some agenda in her actions. She, in turn, studied him for a moment before answering. Perhaps he was only coming on strong to make up for his lack of a commanding presence.

"I'm here to visit my grandmother," she said when his frown announced he had waited long enough.

"Hmmm." Chief Browning leafed through a small notebook, as if checking her response against something. "And how do you know Mrs. Wells?"

"I don't. She came to me for help when her husband collapsed."

The frown deepened. Kate frowned in return. Didn't he believe her? What had Tiff said?

"Mrs. Wells indicated you intended to move here."

"I'm considering it." She almost stopped there, to make him work to pull information out of her, but decided it might not be smart to anger this police chief. "My grandmother is getting on in years and may need a family member nearby to look after her interests."

The look Chief Browning gave her clearly indicated he was dubious about her intentions.

"All right," he said, "give me your version of what happened tonight."

My version? Taking a deep breath to control the temper that was always too close to the surface, she recounted what had happened from the time Tiffany Wells banged on her door.

"So, after she called 911, you are saying Mrs. Wells knocked on the door of a complete stranger looking for help?"

"That's what she said."

"And you believed her?"

"Why wouldn't I?"

Chief Browning stuffed the notebook in his pocket, pulled the cigar out of his mouth, and leaned forward to put his face close to hers. "She left her suffering and possibly dying husband, even after calling 911. Did she go to the office, where there might actually be someone who could help her? No, she goes next door to a complete stranger. Why do you suppose she did that?"

Kate stepped back, narrowing her eyes. What was he implying? "I have no idea."

"Have you ever spoken to Mrs. Wells before tonight?" he asked.

"No. I already told you, I never met her before." Her voice sounded strident to her ears. This was getting ridiculous.

"Are you sure? Remember, it is easy to trace phone connections these days."

"I'm sure," Kate spat out. Her hands were now balled into fists at her sides.

"Where did you eat dinner tonight?"

Where did that question come from? She glared at him. They were both distracted by the sound of her stomach rumbling. "I didn't have a chance to eat dinner. And I'd like to rectify that as soon as possible."

Chief Browning studied her for a long time. "I am finished for now, Ms. Christensen. But stay around. This is not over."

She almost asked why. He was definitely acting as if Phil's death was not an accident. Even if it wasn't, she doubted he could force her to stay in town. But, since she was going to anyway, she decided it was best to inform him. "I'll be moving into my vacation rental tomorrow. After that, I'm not going anywhere for a while."

He took the address of the rental, gave her a final frown, and strode to his car.

Kate looked across the street at the ZigZag Café. If Chief Browning wanted to know where she had eaten, they must have determined Phil died from food poisoning. When she thought about it, though, she realized it happened awfully fast, and it seemed strange that Tiff wasn't also affected. Is that why the chief pulled his car into the café's parking lot and joined the others inside?

She went to the motel's check-in counter where, because of all the commotion, the young man was still on duty. "Is there another restaurant within walking distance?" she asked.

"Not very close, no. There is a Wendy's up the

street, about half a mile. The ZigZag serves real good food, though."

Kate shuddered. She was too tired to walk anywhere. She considered driving; that wasn't a good idea, even for only half a mile, after the amount of bourbon she had consumed.

Returning to her motel room, she found Tiff hunched in the chair, wrapped in a blanket. "That policeman sort of searched the room," she whispered. "I wonder what he was looking for."

"He what? I don't think he had the right to search my room without a warrant."

"He didn't ask. And he didn't really search through anything. He kind of walked around and looked real close at everything while he questioned me."

Kate waited a moment for her anger to subside. It wasn't Tiff's fault, but she'd like to have a word with Chief Browning. When she had calmed down, she asked, "Did you give an officer the keys to search your car?"

Tiff nodded.

Kate sighed. She supposed that if Tiff gave permission they didn't need a warrant.

"Do you want a pizza?" she asked.

Tiff shuddered. "I don't think I could eat a thing. I guess I'd better get myself another room. I can't stay in that one."

Kate was not comfortable sharing a room, but she couldn't leave the shivering and teary-eyed Tiff alone tonight. "There are two beds in this room. You'll stay here with me," she said. "Can you get your stuff?"

"Oh, thank you." Tiff cried, jumping up and throwing her arms around Kate. She went out and immediately returned, her eyes wide with alarm, before Kate had a chance to order pizza. "There is an officer putting tape over the door. It says crime scene. What does that mean? What crime?"

Kate stared at her. Even though she had also been trying to deny the logical outcome of all the police activity, Tiff was really out of it if she hadn't realized by now that the police found something very wrong with the way Phil died.

Shaking her head, Kate charged out the door and confronted the young officer. "Excuse me," she said in her best Katherine Anne Christensen corporate-attorney voice. "All of Mrs. Wells belongings are in that room. You surely have searched them already and can let her have them before you seal it off."

The officer, who had evidently walked across from the café because the squad car was still there, looked uncertain. He glanced back across the street before grabbing his radio. After a short conversation, he disconnected, relief spreading across his face.

"All right. She had not unpacked her suitcase, and we are finished searching it. I'll get it for you."

When Kate brought the bag into her room, Tiff opened it and jumped back, letting out a small scream. "What a mess!" she cried. "Did they have to do that?"

"Probably not," Kate said, her voice resigned. "They probably didn't even have a right to. At least you have your things. You can wait to get Phil's until they finish over there."

Eventually Tiff fell into a fitful sleep with the help of yet another shot of bourbon. By this time, Kate had given up on ordering pizza and foraged through her travel supplies for any remaining snack food. She took her drink, cell phone, and a tuna-and-cracker snack box along with her last apple out to the picnic table.

Call Mom? Don't call Mom? While she debated, she ate the tuna on cracker and apple as slowly as possible, hoping it would last her until morning. She didn't want to think she always had to call Mommy when things went wrong. She was a big girl. She had worked in the testosterone-laden world of corporate law. She had taken off on her own without consulting Mommy about the move. She could handle this. She could.

But, she *had* taken off on her own without consulting her mother, and she hadn't told her mother what she was doing. It was time to do that. She picked up her cell phone and dialed.

"I'm in Cactus," she announced without preamble when her mother answered.

"What?" Her mother nearly yelped. "Well, good for you," she added after a moment. "I am glad you finally took some time off. But why didn't you tell anyone? Has something happened to your grandmother?"

"No. I haven't even talked to Nana yet." She took a deep breath. "I quit my job." The line was silent so long Kate began to get nervous. She tensed, making herself wait to see how her mother would respond. When Mom finally spoke, her voice was strained.

"Why? And why didn't you talk to me about it?"

If she had, Kate was sure her mother would have tried to talk her out of it, as well as the rest of her plans. With a pang of guilt, she plunged ahead. "And, I'm moving to Arizona."

She hoped her supervisor, Doug, would be as shocked as her mother seemed to be when he opened the envelope she had left on his desk late Friday night, informing him that she was giving a month's notice and taking the month in vacation. She had more than that coming to her, but she hadn't wanted to push it. She hoped Doug would take the hint that she was willing to drop the real reason for her leaving, which would be damaging to both of them.

The firm might pay her for the rest of what it owed her, or it might not pay her at all since she hadn't asked to take vacation or given notice before doing so. She expected Doug would try to make sure she got at least what she asked for so that she wouldn't make any waves. She was sure she had blown any chance of a decent recommendation, though. She didn't care about that. She was finished with corporate life.

She did care about worrying her mother. But Mom was a strong woman. She had weathered the death of Kate's father and gone on to face challenges few people would dream of. She could handle it.

"You are busy with your own life, now that you're adopting Eric and Benjamin," Kate finally said, pleased that she managed to keep any hint of resentment out of her voice. She admired Mom and her new husband, Pete, for what they were doing. Only it made her feel a little bit as if she and her older brother, Robert, had been put on the back burner of their mother's life. "I felt the need to get away quickly, so I packed my bags and took off."

"Is something wrong that you needed to get away so fast? Do you have a place to stay? Do you have any plans for the future? That's a long way from home." Her mother's voice continued to rise as she prattled on in uncharacteristic fashion.

"Yes, I was lucky to find a vacation rental on short notice." Kate almost bit her tongue. Mom was such a stickler for the truth. Kate couldn't tell her she had been planning this for some time and not talked to her about it. "I'm in a motel tonight and I'll move into the vacation rental tomorrow. And, anyway, this isn't as far as you moved away from your family."

"That was different," Mom protested. "I went away to school, and when I met your father we had to make our plans together." Kate heard the sharp intake of breath before she continued. "Is that what happened? Have you met someone special?"

Kate laughed. "No, sorry to disappoint you. Nothing like that." With enough food to calm her stomach and plenty of bourbon in her system, the weight of fatigue made her slump on the bench. "I'm beat, Mom," she said. "I'll talk to you again tomorrow evening, after I get settled and you've had time to digest my news." She disconnected before her mother could object. Tomorrow would be soon enough to fill her in on everything that had happened since she arrived in Cactus City.

Returning to the warmth of the motel room, Kate

glanced at Tiff, sound asleep, her long legs escaped from the covers. Resisting the urge to tuck Tiff in properly, she stripped, pulled an oversized T-shirt over her head, and collapsed into her own bed. Sleep didn't come easily. Too much had happened too quickly, and her mind went into incessant replay.

Was it only this afternoon she had exited a series of hairpin curves that ended abruptly at Cactus City, Arizona? What in the world had made her stop at the Switchback Motel? She tossed to her other side. If she had driven into town, she could have found a larger, name-brand motel. None of this would have happened and she would be looking forward to seeing Nana tomorrow and starting their life together. But she'd had no premonition of what was to come when she checked in at the rustic lobby that adjoined a string of a dozen doors with parking in front of them.

Entering the clean, welcoming room decorated with Native American art, Kate had felt pleased with herself for following her impulse to stop. She flipped over again. How had she become tangled up in this mess? What perverse twist of fate had brought her to this place at this time?

CHAPTER THREE

Tuesday morning Kate's eyes popped open to a moment of panic. Where was she? Her heart beat faster as she clutched the blanket—until she awoke enough to remember that she had quit her job and was safely in the mountains of Arizona.

Taking a deep breath, she settled back into the warm bed, wallowing in the unaccustomed luxury of sleeping in. Her watch, still set on Seattle time, said she was awake an hour later than her usual five o'clock, but the bedside clock said it was actually seven. She didn't have to be out of the motel until eleven and couldn't check into her rental until two, so she had planned on a leisurely lunch and stroll around town, a day to get her bearings before going to see Nana.

Glancing over at the other bed, she saw Tiff's long hair spread over her pillow. Last night's events came flooding back. She shook her head. She had no idea how much Tiff's presence might complicate her plans.

Maybe a run would help her stay grounded, whatever she had to face.

Pulling on running pants and a long-sleeved shirt, she strapped on a water bottle while a pot of coffee brewed. Cup in hand, which she was pleased to note was not Styrofoam, she slipped out of the room and stopped. Her view of the mountains in the moonlight last night hadn't opened up half of the panorama that surrounded the town on three sides. Now the mountains welcomed her. Turning in a circle, she saw that rolling hills covered with brushy greenery, cottonwood trees, and a few prickly pear cacti blocked the view to the west. In all other directions, sharply defined ridges and peaks greeted her.

Breathing deeply, Kate did some stretches while letting the caffeine complete the job of bringing her fully awake. No uppers. Coffee would have to suffice in her new life.

Although the air was still chilly, the sun was already making itself felt as she jogged halfway up a slight slope toward Wendy's restaurant. She passed two paved streets to her left and three dirt roads leading up the hills on her right, before she had to stop and lean over, gasping, to catch her breath. She had forgotten how the altitude would affect her.

Since the motel didn't offer a free breakfast and her stomach was more than ready for some real food, she walked the rest of the way to Wendy's. Seattle offered so many interesting options, she had rarely settled for fast food. After eying the steel-cut oatmeal she was surprised to find on Wendy's menu, she decided to splurge on a sausage and egg burrito and a cup of what turned out to be surprisingly good coffee. She appreciated the many windows in the building as she sat and devoured her breakfast while enjoying the view.

Returning down the slope to the motel at a fast walk, she basked in the sun's warmth on her face. In her room, she discovered Tiff hadn't moved, so she hopped in the shower to warm up and wash her close-cropped brown curls. Color from her father, curls from her mother. Kate was grateful for hair that a quick blow dry fluffed into shape, but it did make it even more difficult for her, a woman of small stature, to be taken seriously in the corporate-law environment. The only other obvious gift from her mother was her green eyes, more startling in Kate's olive complexion than in her mother's redhead tones.

Kate decided it was time to rouse Tiff. "I'm sorry," she said. "We have to leave the motel in a couple of hours and I didn't want you to have to rush. Were you able to sleep at all?"

Tiff sat on the edge of the bed and shook her head, frowning. "Not much. I spent the night trying to think about what I'm going to do now. That policeman wants me to stay in town. I'd like to go stay with Dad and find out what the situation is with this woman he married. I could get back from Phoenix in a couple of hours, but that wasn't good enough for him. He's such a butthead."

Kate giggled at the description. "He wants me to stay in town, too, but I'll be going to my vacation rental today anyway. I'm not sure he can make you stay unless he charges you with something."

Tiff cocked her head, a slight frown on her brow. "Charges me?" She shook her head and sighed. "Anyway, I haven't had a modeling job yet since we moved to San Diego. Phil recently got a good job there and was doing okay, but he hasn't been at it long enough to save much. So, I don't know how long I can pay for a motel."

"Why don't you stay with me for a day or two until you can figure out your finances and the police let you go?" Kate wished the words back before she had finished saying them. She hardly knew this girl. A young woman who appeared to be the center of a murder investigation, a fact that didn't seem to have penetrated Tiff's thinking so far. A person who the police might not let go.

Tiff jumped up, nearly overturning the table. She threw her arms around Kate. "Oh, Katie, thank you so much. You are such a good person. I'll pay you back somehow, I promise."

Katie?

"Wait. You don't need to worry about that now, but remember this will be a one-bedroom unit. You'll have to sleep on the sofa." At Tiff's so-what expression, Kate gave up any hope of rescinding the offer. "Get ready to check out and I'll take you to Wendy's for breakfast. After that, maybe we can do a little sightseeing until the rental is available at two."

Kate stuffed her belongings into her overnight bag. She stopped, her hand hovering over the bag before she zipped it shut. Did she know what she was doing? She had come here to figure out her own life, not get involved in someone else's volatile situation.

Katie?

She closed her eyes. Katherine Anne Christensen. Kate for most of her life, Katherine in her professional life. Who was she now?

Katie. She tried it on. It felt good, free, the way she had felt last night when she arrived at the motel. She raised her chin as she checked the room to make sure she had everything. Katie it was.

And, was she in this with Tiff, whatever "this" was?

Kate ... Katie picked up a map of the area and bro- chures about several local landmarks before she and Tiff checked out of the motel at eleven o'clock. Tiff threw her belongings into her blue Chevy Malibu and joined Kate in her Maserati. At Wendy's, she ordered a breakfast burrito to go so they could have three hours to tour, eat lunch, and maybe do a little grocery shop- ping before they checked in at the vacation rental.

"This Jerome place looks like fun," Tiff said as she ruffled through the brochures.

"Yes, but a little far if Chief Browning wants to see us."

Tiff snorted. "Old butthead can't expect us to wait around at his beck and call."

Kate looked at her. "Actually, I think he can. He is investigating the death of your husband."

Tiff visibly shrank, her shoulders rounding. "Of course. I'm, like, you know, trying to get my mind off of it."

A stirring of misgiving unsettled Kate. Was Tiff as innocent as she seemed? The forlorn look on the girl's face made Kate regret the unkind thought. "Let's take a drive through the mountains a little," she suggested. "Lucie won't let us get lost."

"Lucie?"

Kate—no, she was Katie now—laughed. "Lucie is what I call the genie in my GPS. I tell her where I want to go, and she makes sure I get there. Or, if I get lost, I tell her to take me home and she does that."

Tiff managed a small smile and began to search on the radio until she found a station to her liking. She started swaying to music Kate had never listened to, though Katie might. As they curved around a mountain, the music disintegrated into static. "What a pain," Tiff said, punching until she found a station that would come in clearly. It was playing gospel music. She frowned and punched again.

"Lots of luck with finding a station," Katie said. "You know that as soon as you get good reception on one, we'll go behind another mountain and you will lose it. I do have some CDs in the armrest."

Tiff leafed through the CDs, ignoring the new set of deep valleys and soaring mountains that opened up every time they rounded a curve. Finally, she shoved them all back in the armrest.

"Don't you have anything from the last ten years?" she asked.

Katie bristled at being called out-of-date, but after a moment realized she hadn't bought a new CD in at least five years. When she was in college she had promised herself that would never happen. She would always keep up with the music of the day. But, as busy as her life had become, she had fallen back on the music she knew and loved for relaxation.

"Guess not," she said. "You'll have to educate me."

"You're making fun of me," Tiff pouted.

Katie shook her head. "No, honestly, I'm not. I've fallen behind in the last few years, and I'd like to catch up."

"Wow, look at that," Tiff exclaimed, taking in the scenery for the first time. A wall of boulders loomed to their right and a sheer drop threatened on the left, opening into a wide valley before mountains rose again across the way. Tiff's cell phone rang.

"Hello. What? We're taking a drive in the mountains. Okay, I know we said we'd stay available, and we are, but do we have to be prisoners locked in our rooms?"

She listened a moment.

"All right, all right. We'll head back to Cactus City. It won't take us more than twenty minutes to get there."

"Twenty minutes?" Katie exclaimed when Tiff disconnected. "Do you have any idea how long we have been driving?"

"Um, I guess not. I was too busy looking for music."

"Was that the chief?"

"Yes. He said Phil's cousin Jeffrey is in town and raising a fuss that I didn't tell him about Phil."

Katie almost drove off the road. She regained

control and drove a little farther until she found a pull-over where she could maneuver the car into a U-turn.

"You didn't notify him? Did you tell Phil's father?"

Tiff twisted a strand of hair around a finger. "I didn't know how to tell him Phil was dead. And I couldn't face explaining to him what had happened. I thought the police would do it. And I guess they did, or Jeffrey wouldn't know."

"Seriously?" She couldn't believe Tiff hadn't let Phil's father know immediately. Of course, Katie hadn't thought to ask Tiff if she had made the call before taking her sightseeing—but Katie was not the girl's keeper.

Even without speeding, which Katie refused to do on the sharp curves, they made the trip back to Cactus City in less than twenty minutes. She realized it had taken longer to go up because she had driven slowly in order to enjoy as much of the scenery as she could.

They passed the motel and continued into downtown Cactus City, where they found the two-story brick municipal building, set back from the street, with a strip of parking in front. When they entered the door to the police station, an officer took them through a drab, narrow room with chairs against the outer wall and a window on the opposite side behind which Katie could see someone doing paperwork. The officer took them through a door to the left of the window, which led to a small, windowless room. Chief Browning sat at a long table that had two chairs on each side. Beside him was a tall, striking man with tousled sandy hair and fierce blue eyes. The man jumped to his feet, his chair nearly falling over behind him.

"You!" he barked. "What did you do to Phil?"

Tiff seemed to shrink, her eyes taking on the look of a frightened child. "I didn't do anything," she said in a quivery voice. "We were eating our salads when he suddenly felt sick."

"And you didn't bother to tell me or Uncle Jim what had happened?"

"I was worried what the news would do to Dad."

"Don't you call him Dad. He is not your father any more than that schemer living with him is his wife."

Tiff looked as if she had been slapped. The shock seemed to have awakened something in her, though, because a moment later she stood straight and glared at the man, who Katie assumed was Jeffrey. "I love *Dad* as much as if he were my own father. And he loves me too. Phil and I were planning to take him back to San Diego with us."

"Right. When it looked as if Phil's inheritance was in jeopardy, he suddenly took an interest in his father. I suppose you planned to get rid of the harlot first." Jeffrey's voice dripped with sarcasm. "But you couldn't bother to tell Uncle Jim you murdered his son."

"M...m...murder?" Tiff looked confused.

So, I was right, Katie thought. They have determined Phil was murdered. How though?

"I did not m...m...murder Phil." Tiff shrank again at the accusation.

Chief Browning broke in. "Someone did, and you look like the most likely suspect to me." He leaned his forearms on the table and peered at Tiff through narrowed eyes. "The medical examiner recognized the signs right away, so he checked and found monkshood in his system. Where did you get it?"

Tiff looked even more confused. "Get what?"

"Don't act so innocent. It was no coincidence that you stopped in what you must consider a Podunk little town when you could easily have gone on to Phoenix—was it? You figured the local yokels wouldn't have the smarts to figure out what you did."

Tiffany shook her head back and forth, her eyes wide with shock. "You think I murdered Phil?" she asked in a faint voice. "I couldn't do that. I loved Phil. He was all I had."

"Do you have any proof?" Katie asked, but she felt a sinking in the pit of her stomach. Indeed, as the chief had said, who else could have done it? Who even knew they would stop to eat in Cactus City? Looking for another possibility, she turned on Jeffrey. "Where were you last night?"

"Who are you and what are you doing here?" he demanded.

"I am a friend of Tiff's, and it appears she needs one right now," Katie retorted.

"Well, I was attending a knife-throwing competition, if it's any of your business," he said.

Katie blinked. *A what?* She shook her head.

"And, why would Tiff poison Phil?" she asked.

"For the inheritance when Uncle Jim dies, of

29

course." A crooked grin crossed Jeffrey's face as he turned back to Tiff. "But you blew that, didn't you? You weren't smart enough to come up with a plan you could get away with."

Katie frowned. She hadn't dealt with inheritance law since she was in school. But Phil's father was still alive. What did Phil's inheritance from him have to do with anything? "Was Phil an only child?" she asked.

"Yes. Uncle Jim's next closest relative is my mother, his sister."

"So, now that Phil is dead, wouldn't your mother inherit when her brother dies? Or did your uncle specify Tiff as a beneficiary?"

"Not specifically. He left everything to Phil, or to Phil's heirs if Phil died first."

Katie turned to Tiff. "Did Phil have a will?"

"Yes," she said, her voice small. "He left everything to me. But he didn't have much."

Chief Browning had been watching the interchange without comment. "So," he said, "you are Phil's beneficiary, and when his father dies, you will also get that estate."

Tiff looked confused. "I guess so. We didn't expect Phil to die first, so we didn't think about it." She frowned at Jeffrey. "How did you know anything about Dad's will? I don't know what's in it and I don't know if he ever showed it to Phil."

Jeffrey snorted. "Right," he said. "Who would Uncle Jim be more likely to leave everything to than his only son? It's pretty hard to believe you didn't know."

Katie thought that sounded like someone who resented being left out. "But, Mr. Wells is still alive," she said. "He may change his beneficiary now that Phil is gone. It seems to me it's stretching it a bit to say Tiff murdered Phil for a possible future inheritance."

Chief Browning spoke up. "Ms. Christensen, you may go for now. I need to speak more with Mrs. Wells and Mr. Crane."

"Can't she stay?" Tiff pleaded, her voice small. "I need a friend with me."

"No, not while I'm questioning you." He turned to Katie. "Didn't you say you could move into your rental this afternoon? I'll let you know when I'm ready to talk to you, so don't go gallivanting off again."

Katie bit back a retort, gave Tiff an apologetic look, and forced herself to follow Chief Browning's order. There was nothing she could do for the girl, since she was neither a criminal attorney nor licensed in the state of Arizona.

She wished she could listen in on that interrogation, though, because she was sure that was what it would be. She wondered if Tiff would be allowed to leave at the end of it. Or if she needed to find an attorney.

In about ten minutes her genie, Lucie, had directed Katie back toward the motel, up a dirt road, and around a bend, where the three vacation rental units nestled with two other houses in a space between scrub-oak-covered hills. Parking was to the side of the rentals. She punched in the code the owner had provided to open the mailbox and retrieved the two keys left there for her. It didn't take long to unload her belongings from the car.

Katie's unit only afforded a peek-a-boo view of the hills surrounding it. However, it was completely and pleasantly furnished in tones of beige, green, and copper. A closet was on the left of the entry door, the bedroom and bathroom off to the right. The living room led to a dining area with a spacious kitchen to the right of it. A back door on the other side of the kitchen opened to a small room containing the washer and dryer she would share with the neighboring units.

Satisfied with the accommodations, she proceeded to unpack. The closet at the entry would give Tiff a place to stow her belongings when she got here. A set of sheets on the shelf prompted Katie to check the sofa. She was relieved to discover it was actually a hide-a-bed, which would be much more comfortable for Tiff. The only drawback was that Tiff would have to go through Katie's bedroom to get to the bathroom. Katie didn't want her to be too comfortable, anyway. She hoped Tiff would be gone after a few days so she could go on with her own plans.

Which reminded her it was time to call her grandmother.

The phone rang so long Katie was almost ready to hang up when she heard a thump and a pause. Finally, a quivery voice said, "Hello."

"It's Katie ... Kate, Nana. I'm here, in Cactus City. Are you all right?"

"Oh, I'm so glad you called. I took a fall, and I can't get up."

Katie couldn't find her voice for a moment. "Did you phone for help?" she asked.

"No, I took that necklace with the call button off when I took my shower and forgot to put it back on."

"Um, Nana, you are on the phone now. You could have called 911."

"Oh, can I still do that? I thought I was supposed to use the button. Anyway, the phone rang and I pulled the phone cord to make the receiver fall down to me."

Katie frowned. Her grandmother sounded confused. She evidently didn't remember Katie was coming for a visit. Katie had already suspected Nana's memory was slipping, which was part of the reason she had decided to move nearer to her. But this kind of confusion was unlike the Nana she knew. Maybe it was because of the fall.

"All right, I'm going to disconnect now. I'm going to call 911 and come over. Can you hang up the phone?"

"No. I pulled it down by the cord and I can't reach to put it back up."

Katie had forgotten her grandmother's phone was so old it still had a cord connecting it to the base. She thought Nana could disconnect without hanging up, but she didn't remember for sure. "Don't worry. I'll take care of it when I get there. Is the door locked?"

"Oh, my dear, yes. I always lock my door. How are you going to get in?"

"I'll take care of it. You relax now and leave it to me."

She disconnected and called 911, giving them the address and information about what had happened.

"The door may be locked, but go ahead and get in any way you can," she said, not knowing if they needed permission to break in.

She shivered with worry as she hurried out to the car. Dad had been Nana's only child, so it would be up to her brother, Robert, and her to do whatever needed to be done for their grandmother as she aged. Katie realized that, as busy as she had been with her own life, she had never considered what that might mean in her future.

Despite her determination to leave her former self behind and become "Katie," the efficient Katherine Ann Christensen began to make a mental list of the things she would need to check on. She wouldn't take steps to do anything until after she had seen her grandmother and discovered what her current situation was. She might not need to do anything at all. But, right now, if there was something that needed to be done, she had to figure out how she would go about doing it.

Katie was halfway to Nana's house when her cell phone rang. She didn't usually answer her cell while driving, but a glance at the caller ID told her it came from the police station. "I need you to come in for some further questions now," Chief Browning said.

"I can't come right now, and I shouldn't even be on the phone since I'm driving. I'm on my way to my grandmother's house. She has fallen and can't get up."

"Did you call emergency?"

"Yes, but I said I would be there too. She seems to be confused and won't know what to do."

"I think you'll find our emergency responders know how to handle that situation," the chief said. "You can come in and talk to me now and see your grandmother later."

Katie stared at the phone. Had she heard correctly? What would happen if she ignored him?

"Chief Browning, I should warn you that if you insist I do this now I will be putting in an official complaint that you are abusing the power of your badge. I will answer any questions you want, but I have to see that my grandmother is all right first."

"I wondered how long it would take before you used that fancy legal education of yours to try and keep us from doing our job. Put in any complaints that you want, Ms. Christensen, but get your butt in here right now for questioning." He paused. "Besides, you need to pick up your friend here, since we are finished with her for now."

The line went dead.

Pick up her friend? They must not have any real evidence against her. But Tiff was not Katie's responsibility. Nana was. And if Nana needed her attention now, how was she going to disengage from Tiff's problems?

CHAPTER FOUR

Katie's grandmother lived in a small house at the end of a cul-de-sac off Rodeo Street on the less hilly side of Cactus City. Katie drove up at the same time her call from the police chief ended. EMS and a fire truck were already parked in the circle. Racing to the door, she saw that they had put Nana on a gurney and were rolling her out.

"That was great response time." Katie frowned, looking at the door. "You didn't have to break in?"

"The door was unlocked," a fireman replied.

Katie stored that away to think about later. "Is my grandmother all right? Where are you taking her?"

"The EMTs are taking her to the clinic where they can determine if the fall caused serious enough damage that they need to send her to the hospital in Prescott."

"Good," Katie said. "Nana, where are your keys?"

"Hanging by the door." Her voice was weak and spidery.

"All right, I'll lock up. There is something I have to do right now, but I'll get to the clinic as soon as I can."

Katie raced into the house, checked to make sure someone had replaced the phone on its base, took a quick look to ensure everything else was in order, locked the door, and in moments was back in her car heading to the police station. Her cell phone rang again. She ignored it.

"Where the hell have you been?" Chief Browning demanded when she entered the police station five minutes later.

"What? I got here as fast as I could. I don't know the streets in this town. And I don't appreciate you swearing at me."

Chief Browning looked confused for a moment. Katie hid a grin. He obviously hadn't been brought up in a church that considered "hell" a swear word.

With a shake of his head, he continued. "Ms. Christensen, we need to go over again your acquaintance with Mrs. Wells and what you know about this whole situation."

Katie looked around. They were still standing in the entry of the station. Jeffrey and Tiff sat side by side on chairs against the wall. Katie's eyes were drawn to Jeffrey, leaning back in his chair with his arms folded, one ankle resting on his knee. His deep frown distorted the rugged good looks of his face. Tiff looked pale and drawn. She seemed unaware of anything around her. Two other chairs were occupied by men evidently waiting for something or someone.

"I don't have anything to add to what I told you before," Katie said. "But I'm puzzled. I couldn't be here when you questioned Tiffany, which you did in a private room, but we can be out here for everyone to listen while you interrogate me?"

The two men glanced up, eyes sharp with interest.

"Why should that bother you? You claim you have nothing to tell me."

Katie shook her head. She wished she could record this. Who would believe it otherwise? "Ask away," she said.

"How long have you known Tiffany Wells?"

"Since she knocked on my motel door last night."

"And yet, you invited her to live with you."

"I invited her to stay with me for a few days because you demanded she remain in town and she has no place to stay. I don't think you are going to pay for a motel room, and I'm not sure what her financial situation is."

"If you aren't acquainted with Mrs. Wells, how is that your problem?"

"Human decency, Chief Browning. Something you seem to know little about."

The storm clouds darkening the chief's light-brown eyes told Katie she may have gone too far. But what could he do, really? She was telling the truth, so there was no way he could accuse her of anything and make it stick. Still, she was glad there were witnesses to what was going on.

"What were you two concocting during your drive up in the mountains today?"

"How she is going to update my taste in music."

The chief's fists clenched and Katie had the distinct impression that if there were no witnesses present he would have struck her.

"Chief Browning, if you have nothing of any significance to ask me, I need to get to the clinic, where my grandmother was taken after a fall today. Which you knew about before you insisted I come in here for these absurd questions." She figured that as long as she had an audience, she might as well milk it.

The chief glanced at the two very interested men seated beside Jeffrey and Tiff. "I did not know your grandmother was injured enough to be taken to the clinic." His voice sounded tight, with barely controlled rage. "Of course, you may go." He paused. "I have half a notion to lock Mrs. Wells up right now."

"With what evidence?" Katie demanded.

"She was the only one around."

"So, you want to arrest her for being with her husband when he died?" She rolled her eyes. "Well, I can't think of anyone else, so why don't I arrest you?"

The chief made a distinct growling sound. "You may both go," he said. "I will call you back if I have more questions."

"What?" Jeffrey jumped to his feet. "Aren't you going to lock up that b...." He glanced at Katie. "Witch for murdering my uncle?"

So, Jeffrey *had* been brought up in a church that banned bad words.

"Probably. But not until we have enough evidence to make it stick."

"Why don't you go to your grandmother?" Tiff asked when they left the station. "I can get a cab to the motel and drive to your place. I need to make a stop on the way."

"No, I'll take you. It isn't far. I have the extra key to the unit to give you, though, so if you can find your way there, I'll leave you at the motel and go see my grandmother."

After dropping Tiff off, Katie asked Lucie for directions to the clinic and arrived at the adobe building on a flat parcel of land south of Main Street five minutes later. She rushed in, hardly noticing her surroundings, and found her grandmother in an emergency room cubicle, looking a little dazed and confused.

"I only needed someone to help me get up," she complained, her voice whiny. "Why did they have to bring me here?"

"Now, Mrs. Christensen," a nurse said. "You know we had to do some tests and check for a concussion and broken bones."

"So, did you find any?"

Katie was surprised at the quick change to sharpness in her grandmother's tone. Her mother had always told Katie she got her temper from this grandmother. She could see why.

"I don't believe so."

"So, Kate can take me home?"

"We'll have to wait for the doctor to discharge you."

Nana laid back, looking defeated. "That could take hours," she said.

Katie grinned and sat in the chair beside the bed

to wait. "I've changed my name," she said, hoping to distract her grandmother.

"Really?" Nana said, more strength in her voice now. "Why?"

"I'm ready to change my life and I thought Katie was more in tune with my new personality."

"So, you can change your personality just like that?"

Katie was pleased to see a weak grin pass over Nana's face. "Maybe not. But I can change the way I live my life."

"What was wrong with the old one? I thought you were happy there."

"I was, for a while. But it got to be too much." Katie knew she needed some kind of explanation for her grandmother. She had already decided how much she would divulge. "There was so much stress I couldn't sleep, and then I couldn't focus on my work. I got in the habit of taking uppers in the morning to give me energy and downers at night so I could sleep. Some of my coworkers started using cocaine. They said it made them feel sharper and they could accomplish more. I tried it a couple of times, and it worked, but I worried when I saw them using more and more. I decided I didn't want to go down that path, so I opted out."

"Thank God you did," Nana said. "It would be terrible to lose you to drugs. What does your mother think about you changing your life?"

"I didn't ask her. She's busy with the two boys she and Pete are adopting and I didn't want to worry her. After I got here, I called and told her I had quit my job and moved to Cactus City." Katie was glad her grandmother was satisfied with her answer. There was more to her leaving but she didn't want to get into it right now ... if ever.

"Moved here?" Nana sounded delighted before her eyes clouded over. "I don't know what you'll find here that will use your talent and education." She frowned. "So, your mother has forgotten about Gene and started herself a new family."

"No, no, Nana. Mom would never forget Dad. But Pete is a great guy who she says makes her life whole again."

"I never needed anyone new after your grandfather died."

Katie was spared the need to respond by the arrival of the physician's assistant.

"You were fortunate this time, Mrs. Christensen. No broken bones and the test results that have come back are normal. There still could be problems we haven't identified, though, so you need to make an appointment with Dr. Pelson to follow up." He glanced at Katie. "Are you staying with Mrs. Christensen?"

Katie shook her head. "I am her granddaughter. I am in the process of moving to Cactus City, but her house is too small for me to stay with her."

"I've given your grandmother something to help with pain. It should last about six hours, but we have to be careful about medication until we have more information about her condition, especially the bump on her head. Can you make sure she doesn't take more than the dose on the package I'm giving her?"

Katie nodded, hoping she could manage that. Before her grandmother had time to object to being monitored, he continued. "When she arrived, we asked her to fill out the paperwork to name someone as her health power of attorney. She named you."

"Am I a child?" Nana fumed as soon as he left the room. "I'm perfectly capable of taking care of myself."

While Nana still looked frail and a bit shaky, it was good to see her spunk had returned. "We'll talk about all that stuff later," Katie said. "Let's get you home."

When she had entered her grandmother's house earlier, Katie had been rushed and hadn't looked around carefully. Her heart sank when she did so now. It was obvious her grandmother's eyesight wasn't what it used to be or she would not have allowed the layer of dust that coated everything in the tiny living room. The dishes had been washed and stacked in the drainer to dry, but streaks of food remained on them.

"I'm sorry about the mess," Nana said, removing several magazines from a chair. "I wasn't expecting company."

Katie's grandmother had moved into this house shortly after her grandfather died. She said there were too many memories in her old house, but Katie thought finances might have also played a role in the move. It was definitely a house for one, more like a dollhouse than a place where people lived. The bathroom was the width of the bathtub and barely deep enough to accommodate a sink and toilet next to the head of the tub. There were two rooms in the back, both inadequate to be called bedrooms. Nana had her bed in one and a dressing area in the other. While it had a kitchen, living room, and dining area, they were all so small it was hard to move around the furniture.

Katie had missed lunch; she suspected Nana had too. An early eater, Nana was probably ready for dinner. Checking the refrigerator, Katie couldn't find anything from which to make a decent meal.

"What were you planning on eating, Nana?"

"Oh, whatever I could find. I have some tuna fish, and soup."

"Would you like to go out to eat?" She knew the answer even before she asked.

"No, that would be too much after the day I've had."

"I'm going to call a new friend of mine and see if she wants to pick up something and eat with us," Katie said.

When she called, Tiff said she had an upset stomach and didn't feel up to going out again. Katie fought off a surge of resentment. She had to remember Tiff was having a rough time right now. She checked the phone book for area restaurants and was pleased to see a KFC not far away. "Would you like a hamburger or something from KFC?" she asked.

Nana's face brightened. "Oh, a chicken pot pie would be wonderful."

As she drove to the restaurant, Katie decided that she needed to learn how to cook. For the last few years, dinner had been whatever she could order or pick up in a hurry, but at least in Seattle there were multiple choices of cuisine to choose from. She couldn't imagine feeding her grandmother a steady diet of fast food, which seemed to be the only take-out available.

"I'll bet you're ready for a good night's sleep," Katie said when they had finished eating and she was putting most of Nana's pot pie in the refrigerator. "Why don't you go to bed and I'll get settled into my rental place? I'll be back tomorrow to see how you're doing. I'm going to leave another of the pills the physician's assistant gave us in case you wake up with aches and pains in the middle of the night. Will you be all right?"

"Oh, yes. I have everything I need. Don't you worry about me."

But worry is what Katie did while she drove to the vacation rental. When she walked in, she found Tiff lying on the couch, her belongings piled in the living room.

"Um, the closet, here, is for you," Katie said.

"Did you bring back anything to eat?" Tiff asked.

"No, it didn't sound like you wanted anything. Have you eaten anything since we left the police station?"

"I had an energy bar. I had other things on my mind."

"Well, I'm sorry. If I had known, I would have stopped for something. I thought we'd go grocery shopping in the morning, but we could go now if you want."

Tiff made a face. "No, that's all right. I probably couldn't eat, anyway. I'm not feeling hungry."

"Well, if you're sure." Katie paused a minute. "Have you called your father-in-law?"

"What good will that do? I can't go to Phoenix to see him."

"Phil's cousin must have spoken to your father-in-law, so he knows you're here. He'll probably be upset that you haven't called. I'm sure the police can't stop you from doing a day trip to see him."

Tiffany scowled. "I don't think old butthead wants me to do that." She shook her head. "I'm so confused. Someone killed Phil and that policeman thinks I did it? How could I? I loved Phil. Now I have no one—nothing. What if Phil's father doesn't want to have anything to do with me now that Phil is gone?"

Katie shook her head. Tiff seemed to equate love with being taken care of. "Even if he doesn't, you told Chief Browning you loved Phil's father as if he were your own dad. Don't you think it would seem a little strange if you didn't want to go see him?"

Tiff's face brightened. "Oh. You mean, like, he won't let me go, but it will look good for me that I want to?"

"You do want to—don't you?" Katie asked.

"Of course, I do. It's, like, I've been feeling a little sick the last couple of days, and I don't know if I could drive by myself to Phoenix."

Katie's eyes narrowed. Tiff had an answer for every-thing. Was she as naïve as she seemed? Did she really care about Phil's father, or was it all an act? "Even if you don't go see him, you definitely should talk to him."

What was Katie doing? By telling Tiff what she thought an innocent person would do in the circumstances, was she helping the girl build a case for herself?

CHAPTER FIVE

Before going to bed, Katie did a search on Dr. Pelson and the clinic in Cactus City. The results were encouraging. Dr. Pelson, with the help of a large donation and ongoing fundraising efforts, had established the Cactus City Clinic with far more than the usual clinic capabilities in order to serve this isolated community for all but the most critical medical needs. Relieved that Nana would be able to get good care close to home, Katie was able to fall into a deep sleep for the rest of the night.

Tiff was still burrowed into the covers when Katie emerged from her room the next morning. "I have to check on my grandmother today," Katie said. "Let's get a bite to eat and pick up groceries first."

"You go," Tiff moaned. "I don't feel up to it."

Resentment stirring again, Katie skipped going to Wendy's and picked up bread, soup, eggs, and a few other essentials at the small grocery in town. Tiff was up and had showered by the time she returned, but still looked pale and drawn. Katie prepared boiled eggs and toast for their breakfast.

"What are you going to do today?" she asked.

Tiff shrugged her shoulders. "I don't know. Could I go along with you?"

Katie had enough to do to take care of her grandmother. Was she going to have to take care of Tiff too? "Don't you have arrangements to make? When they release Phil's body you'll have to let them know what funeral home will be handling things, and you need to arrange with the funeral home for whatever services you want. And, if you don't already know, you need to find out what resources you and Phil have that are available to you right now."

"I think Phil made arrangements with a funeral home in San Diego to make sure his body would be sent to Phoenix for burial. But all those papers are back in our apartment in San Diego."

"Do you know the name of the funeral home?"

"Yes."

"Start there. They can help you figure out what to do and when. So, do you plan to move back to San Diego?"

Tiff shuddered. "No. At least not to that apartment. I could never live in it without Phil. And I was only in San Diego because of his job. I might be a little old to continue modeling ... right now, I don't have any idea what to do."

Katie shook her head. "I'm sure they need models of all ages, in all cities. My guess is you'd have no trouble finding work. Anyway, you need to give notice at the apartment and make arrangements for your furnishings. Would you consider moving to Phoenix, to be near Phil's father?"

"That would be a good thing to do, wouldn't it? I need to talk to Dad to see if we can work something out."

"I know you are in mourning over Phil's death," Katie said, trying to sound sincere. She knew no such thing. Tiff looked tired and strained, but she didn't show any signs of mourning. But, to be fair, she might still be in shock.

Leaving Tiff to handle her affairs, Katie drove to the local grocery for a repeat of oatmeal, bread, eggs, soup, and a few other items before going to Nana's. When she walked in the house she found, as she had feared, that her grandmother had not taken the pain pill during the night and hadn't been able to get out of bed this morning. Katie was thankful she'd had the presence of mind to take a key to the house when she left last night.

Katie helped Nana to the bathroom to take care of the essentials and clean up as best she could. After getting Nana to eat a few bites of oatmeal and giving her a painkiller, she settled Nana in her comfortable recliner and tackled the half-cleaned dishes in the kitchen.

"If you had a stroke and couldn't make decisions for yourself, who would make them for you?" she asked.

"I presume your brother, Robert. Since your father died, he is the next in line."

"Have you made a power of attorney for him to do that?"

"Why no, I don't think so. I didn't know I needed to."

Katie doubted that her grandmother had made any arrangements. "You need to name someone to handle things when you aren't able to make your own decisions. Do you have an attorney?"

"Well, that nice Mrs. Andrews took care of everything when your grandfather died."

"Oh, good." At least I have a starting place, Katie thought. "We need to talk with Mrs. Andrews. Where do you keep her phone number?"

"It's somewhere on the desk."

Katie eyed the desk as she finished cleaning the dishes. Well, she guessed that was as good a place as any to try to put some order back into Nana's life.

The further Katie got in sorting the papers strewn across the desk, the more worried she became. When the advertisements and requests for donations were cleared out, the stack of unpaid bills and warning notices remaining was alarmingly high. It looked as if her grandmother was lucky to still have heat, lights, and water. Fortunately, Katie found papers showing that Social Security, Nano's pension payments, and the required minimum distribution from a 401(k) plan were all automatically deposited in Nana's account. She had plenty of money.

Looking through the desk, Katie found Nana's checkbook. The last bank statement showed a sizable balance. Since there was no indication any of it had been spent since the statement came out, Katie wrote checks to cover the outstanding bills.

"Oh, I meant to take care of those. I got a little behind," Nana said when Katie gave her the checks to sign. "Thank you so much for doing it."

Once the checks were in the mailbox, Katie looked for Mrs. Andrews' phone number in Nana's address book. It wasn't there. She searched through the desk until she found the attorney's business card, along with several others scattered among an assortment of papers Katie was certain she should look into soon. She frowned, unsettled by what she was discovering. She had used her grandmother's possible need for help as a reason to choose Cactus City as her new home. She hadn't known how right she was. Becoming a full-time caregiver certainly wasn't what she had been expecting.

"Mrs. Andrews," she said when the attorney's receptionist put her through. "My name is Katie ... Katherine Christensen. I arrived in Cactus City yesterday to see my grandmother, Lillian Christensen. When I called her, she was on the floor of her house, unable to get help. Today I discovered her financial affairs are in disarray. I understand she is your client, so I need to get together with you to see what arrangements she has made for her future care."

"Lillian Christensen? Hold on a moment, let me check," a clipped voice replied.

A few minutes later she came back on the line. "Yes, I helped your grandmother get everything transferred to her name after her husband died. I haven't been in contact with her since that time. I understood she had no children."

"Her only child, my father, died some time before my grandfather did, so my brother and I are all the family she has. Right now, I am most concerned with whether she has designated a power of attorney or set up any kind of guardianship if she needs it."

"I'm glad you are looking into her affairs. As far as I can tell, Lillian has made no such arrangements. Would you be the person who would handle things for her?"

"I don't know. It would probably be either my older brother, Robert, or me if she hasn't designated anyone else."

After a short silence, Mrs. Andrews said, "Find out what you can. I agree we should get together. I have an hour open tomorrow afternoon at two."

"Thank you, we'll see you then," Katie said.

Disconnecting, she told her grandmother about the appointment and checked the address book for Nana's doctor. She was elated when she found a listing for Dr. Pelson.

"It looks as if Dr. Pelson is already your doctor," Katie said. "I'm going to call his office, but they won't give me any information. You need to make an appointment to see him. Is that all right?"

At Nana's nod, she punched in the number and handed her the phone. From this end of the conversation, Katie realized it would be two weeks before they would see the doctor. She took the phone.

"Hello? This is Mrs. Christensen's granddaughter. We really need for her to see the doctor as soon as possible. She was taken to the clinic yesterday afternoon after a nasty fall and I found her apartment in disarray when I arrived. The PA at the clinic is still monitoring her condition, but he said my grandmother should see Dr. Pelson as soon as possible."

"The doctor does have a short break in appointments at four o'clock tomorrow. He wouldn't have time for a complete workup, but he could see how she is doing and decide on any further tests."

"Thank you," Katie said. "That's a place to start."

As soon as Katie hung up, her cell phone rang.

"Ms. Christensen, where is your friend Tiffany Wells?" Chief Browning's voice demanded.

"If she's not at my rental, I don't know."

"She's not there. Try again."

A niggle of worry crept through Katie, followed by irritation that this woman she didn't really know was interfering with her life yet again. "Chief Browning, I left her there this morning with the suggestion she contact Phil's father and start making funeral arrangements for Phil. I have been with my grandmother all day."

"Right. Well, when you see her, you can tell her that if she took her car to clean it, she's too late. I had it searched again yesterday, while it was still at the motel. I had to wait for tests on what we found. Guess what it was?"

"I have no idea," Katie said, her stomach clenching at the chief's smug voice.

"A little baggie of that weed that killed her husband, that's what. We now have the evidence we need to arrest her for his murder."

"Wait a minute," Katie objected. "Didn't you already search Tiff's car right after Phil died? You didn't find anything at that time."

"That's right. But I decided we needed to do a more thorough search. My officer evidently missed it the first time."

"What made you decide to search again?" Katie asked.

"Never you mind. But, it's a good thing we did."

"You realize that car was sitting in the motel parking lot all day. It wouldn't have been too hard for someone to plant that stuff in it."

"Now, who would want to do that?"

"Whoever really did kill Phil."

Katie could almost see the smirk on the chief's face when he said, "You're stretching now, Ms. Christensen."

The line went dead.

CHAPTER SIX

Katie managed to spend another half hour with her grandmother even though her mind was on the new revelation about Tiff. Before leaving, she scooped the filling from last night's chicken pot pie into a bowl, ready to be warmed in the microwave. She hoped Nana would remember to eat, but reminded herself that Nana had managed this long without someone watching over her every minute. Katie had other problems to attend to.

When she arrived back at the vacation rental, a police car blocked the parking spaces provided for the renters and Tiff's car was not in sight. By the time she bullied the young officer into letting her park, Katie was steaming.

"You can't go in there," he said, sounding apologetic. "The chief is getting a search warrant."

"Excuse me?" Katie said. "I can't go in my own residence because the chief is *getting* a search warrant? I don't think that quite tracks. When he gets it, let me know."

She almost felt sorry for the officer, but her fury at Chief Browning made her push past the young man and go into the unit.

Nothing had changed since morning. Tiff's possessions were still a jumble in the middle of the living room and none of the groceries Katie had bought had been used. She wondered how long after she had gone to her grandmother's Tiff decided to leave. Where had she gone? Katie wished she had the number for Phil's father. From their morning conversation, she would bet that's where Tiff was, but she had no way to find out. And maybe that was good. If she could honestly tell the chief she didn't know where Tiff had gone, maybe he would get off her case.

She wouldn't bet on it.

The odor of his cigar alerted Katie to Chief Browning's arrival. She turned to the doorway, where he loomed with his customary glare. He flipped the search warrant toward her and started pulling it back, ordering her out.

"You searched everything at the motel," she objected as she grabbed the warrant out of his hand. "How did you get the judge to issue a warrant for another search?"

"This is my town," he said. "Now, you get out of here." The warrant appeared to be valid, so Katie had no option but to obey.

When the police had finished their search, Katie returned and gasped. Not only had Tiff's possessions been strewn about the living room, but her own clothes had been pulled from closets and drawers and were now lying helter-skelter about the bedroom. She looked at the search warrant, sure that Chief Browning had violated its limits. Frowning, she realized the wording was so vague it would be useless to challenge it. It didn't make any difference, anyway, because there was nothing to be found in her room. More important, right now, was to figure out where Tiff had gone and why.

"If I find out you know where she is, you are in big trouble."

Katie jumped. She hadn't heard or smelled the chief return to the doorway.

"I don't know where she is." Katie bit her tongue. Of course, she was going to try and find out where Tiff was, get an explanation from her, but she didn't want the chief to know that.

"Keep your nose out of it then," Chief Browning said, as if reading her thoughts. "This is a police matter and we don't need you meddling in it."

Katie stared after him as he turned and strode back to his car. Had he checked her background? It sounded as if he knew her mother routinely meddled in police investigations. Well, no such luck, Chief Bu...Duck-head, she thought. I'm not my mother, so you'll have to solve your own murder. I only want to make sure Tiff's rights are protected.

But since Katie was a corporate attorney, not a

criminal one, she'd have to figure out how to do that. Or if Tiff even wanted her to. Or if Tiff was someone she should be trying to protect. She needed to talk with Tiff. The police were now building a case on what sounded like real evidence.

Before she started looking, she put her room in order. After that, she began sorting Tiff's belongings. She hung the clothes that she could in the closet and stacked the rest on the shelf.

When she had finished with the clothing, she heated some water for tea. While it was brewing, she put the toiletries in the bathroom and Tiff's other personal items in a drawer in the sofa's end table. Once she had a mug of tea, she sat down at the dining table with what remained.

There wasn't much. Tiff had brought a few photos of herself with Phil, and the two of them with an older gentleman Katie assumed was Phil's father. No photos of her own family. For some reason, she had brought a copy of her marriage license. Katie was surprised the police hadn't taken it. It could show that Tiff was ready to claim her relationship to Phil should it be challenged. Of course, in all that mess, it might have been overlooked.

Overlooking was easily done, she thought, holding an envelope in her hand. She had almost missed the fact that the name on the return address was James Wells. The envelope was empty, but at least the address gave Katie a start in locating Phil's father.

She booted up her laptop, logged in with the Wi-Fi code provided by the rental management, and

Googled James Wells. Sure enough, there were three entries with that name, one at the address on the envelope. She wrote the phone number on the envelope.

She tried the number but got no answer. She tried Tiff's cell phone, too, with the same result. Was Tiff with Jim Wells? Was she avoiding contact? What was she up to?

A pounding at the door made Katie jump and her heart race. "Police! Open the door!" a loud voice, unmistakably Chief Browning's, shouted.

"I'm coming!" she called, hurrying to the door and flinging it open. "You don't have to announce yourself to the whole neighborhood."

The chief shoved his way in and looked around. "Well, you've cleaned everything up nicely. What did you hide while you were doing it?"

"You were here first," she snapped. "And I'd like to know what in that search warrant made you think you could trash my belongings."

"How were we to know what was whose?" He eyed the envelope Katie still held. "What do you have there?"

"You already searched," she retorted. "Do you think you missed something?"

The chief grabbed the envelope out of her hand and studied the address. "My men must have missed this. Where is the letter it contained?"

"I don't know. This is all I found."

"Ms. Christensen, I am this close to arresting you for obstruction of justice. We have a warrant out for the arrest of Tiffany Wells, and it would be in your best interests to cooperate in helping us find her."

"You know as much as I do," Katie replied, shaken by the fact they had put a warrant out on Tiff. "Maybe more, since you searched her belongings before I did."

Chief Browning hitched up his pants and began ruffling through the papers Katie had sorted out from the rest of Tiff's possessions.

"What are you doing? You already searched. Are you making a new mess out of spite?"

"Our search warrant is still in effect," he said, holding up Tiff and Phil's marriage license. "I wonder why your friend thought it necessary to bring this with her?"

"I have no idea. Take it if you want. She can get more copies from *proper* legal authorities if she needs them."

"Make no mistake, Ms. Christensen," Chief Browning said as he turned to leave. "I am the *proper* legal authority in this town."

Katie leaned against the door when he was gone, waving a hand in front of her face to dissipate the odor of cigar smoke. She sank to a squat. Of course, he was right, and there was nothing she could do about it.

She let herself wallow in despair for at least thirty seconds before she stood and squared her shoulders. She would find something to do about it. She didn't know how, but she would. The first thing was to find Tiff.

She still had Jim Wells' information on her laptop,

so she tried Mr. Wells' number and Tiff's cell again. No response. "Please, Tiff," she said into the voicemail recorder. "I want to help if I can, but I need to know what is going on. The police have a warrant out for your arrest, so the Phoenix police will also be looking for you. Is that where you are?"

She shook her head when she disconnected and took a deep breath. She needed to erase Tiff's problems from her mind. There was nothing she could do about them now. Katie needed to start taking care of her own business.

———

She punched Robert's number on her phone.

"Hey," Robert said when he answered. "I hope you know what you are doing. Mom is really worried."

"I do know what I'm doing, Robert," she said. "You don't know how close I was to getting into cocaine with my coworkers. And I had a feeling Nana needed me. I was right."

"Whoa. I do understand the drug issue. I haven't been without temptations myself, especially when I was going through my divorce. I'm glad you separated yourself from that, even though I think you'll regret taking such drastic measures. But, Nana? What about her?"

Katie told Robert about Nana's fall and the worrisome things she had discovered at Nana's house. "She's back home now and doesn't seem to have suffered any permanent damage. I have appointments tomorrow with the attorney who worked with Nano to set things up before he died and with the doctor who runs the clinic. I'm worried about what I can do if she isn't capable of making decisions for herself."

"Are you sure it's that bad?" Robert asked. "She seemed all right when I stopped there during a business trip a few months ago."

"I'm sure it's that bad. She indicated that she assumed you would be the one to make decisions for her, since you are the oldest living relative. But I don't know if she has made anything official. Do you?"

"No, I haven't seen anything like that. Since you're there now, it would probably be easier for you to take it on, if you're willing to."

Katie frowned. "Of course, I'm willing. But if she doesn't want me to handle her affairs, I'll have to go to court to petition for guardianship. I'm sure she would hate that."

Robert didn't speak for a moment. "You're right," he finally said. "Why don't you call me again tomorrow? We'll have a better idea of what needs to be done after you talk with her attorney and doctor. If you need me to come for any reason, you know you only need to ask."

Katie breathed a sigh of relief. "Thank you, Robert." Thank God for her big brother.

"But, about Mom," he added.

Katie stiffened.

"She really is worried about you. Can you find some way to ease her mind? She doesn't need any more stress right now."

"Right now, since she has another family to worry about?" Katie snapped before she had time to stop her tongue.

"That's not fair, Kate. The fact that she and Pete care enough about two at-risk boys to take them into our family doesn't mean she cares any less about us. Olivia and I hope we can all embrace them."

Katie was grateful she managed to stop her tongue this time. Olivia, a social worker who was the case-worker for Mom's two foster sons, was the best thing that had ever happened to Robert, and if that meant Katie had to put up with a little "do-gooder" in her nature, so be it.

"I'll get back to you tomorrow evening," she said.

After disconnecting, she sat at the table and drummed her fingers, her mind drawn back to Tiff. Katie felt an urge to jump into her Maserati and head for Phoenix, but she was quite certain Chief Browning would find some pretext to arrest her if she did. Besides, she wasn't responsible for Tiff. She was supposed to be looking for a job and a place to live. Her cashed out retirement funds wouldn't last her long if she didn't have a paycheck.

When Dad died and left Mom with nothing, Mom sold their family home and Dad's BMW, learned how to invest what she had, resurrected her art talent, and worked whatever minimum-wage job she could get until she ended up with the framing shop.

She glanced out the window at her Maserati.

No! She needed wheels, after all.

That is a pretty expensive set of wheels, she

reminded herself. But, she had worked hard to be able to have a car like that.

Katherine Ann Christensen had worked hard, and it was the right car for her. The idea of selling it felt like a permanent change to her identity. Was she ready for that? She took a sip of cold tea.

If she didn't find work soon, she would have no choice. Rebooting her laptop, she logged onto a job-search site for the Cactus City area. An hour later she sat back, discouraged. Katie would be glad to take one of the available jobs for the time being, but she could imagine what an employer would think about hiring a woman with a law degree for a minimum-wage position. The work that held any potential interest for her required education and experience specific to the field. While she was sure it wouldn't take long to pick up the required knowledge for most of them, she didn't have time to go back to school before earning again. She blinked and looked closer. Even dishwashing required experience.

Come on, Katie, you can figure this out. How did Mom get started? With a bachelor's in applied arts degree and no experience, a prospective employer might not have considered her overqualified. Still, she started with a temporary job. Katie turned back to the computer. A search on temporary jobs didn't look any more promising.

Maybe the temporary agencies had jobs Katie couldn't find online. She accessed the site of the first agency she found in Prescott and pulled up the application form. Struggling with what to enter for "type of work desired," she finally settled on administrative, typing, and legal aid, hoping that was enough to get her in the door so she could actually talk with someone.

Before getting ready for bed, Katie called her grandmother. There was no answer. She stood, gripping her phone, trying to decide what to do. She couldn't keep running back and forth to check on Nana. She couldn't live in that tiny house either. Besides, she had already paid for two months on this vacation rental.

Katie knew she wouldn't be able to sleep unless she was sure Nana was all right. She gathered a few items, added her laptop, and headed out. Tomorrow she'd figure out what to do next.

When she arrived, the house was dark. She let herself in and switched on a light. Nana was still where she had left her, in her recliner, sound asleep. The dinner Katie had prepared before leaving had not been touched.

Katie squatted down beside Nana's chair and gently rubbed her arm. "Nana? Nana? Can you wake up?"

It was a few moments before her eyelids fluttered and opened.

"Katie? What are you doing here?" Her voice was thin and whispery.

"I came to see how you are doing. I'll bet you need to get up and use the bathroom."

"Why, yes, I guess I do. Will you help me?"

"Of course, I will."

Once Nana was on her feet, she seemed steady enough to go to the bathroom without help. While she was gone, Katie decided she might have better luck getting Nana to eat some chicken noodle soup. She found a can in the cupboard, added a little of the pot pie filling, and put it in the microwave to warm. When Nana returned, Katie sat her at the table and placed a bowl of the soup in front of her.

"I'm not very hungry," Nana said.

"Of course, you're not." Katie was certain she was eating so little that she never felt hungry any more. "But take a few bites anyway."

Katie was pleased that Nana managed about half a bowl before declaring she couldn't eat another bite. Katie helped her to bed and collapsed into the recliner. She didn't know if Nana had been this way for a while or whether the fall had sent her over the edge, but Katie knew she shouldn't be left alone. Maybe she would improve, but right now, she needed twenty-four-hour a day monitoring, and this house could not accommodate two people. What was Katie going to tell Robert?

Closing her eyes to think about it, she opened them to the ringing of her cell phone. Tiff's number was on the display. Blinking, Katie looked around. Daylight was shining through the window. She had fallen asleep and slept through the night in Nana's chair.

"Tiff?" she asked. "Where are you?"

"I'm at your rental," she said, her voice high. "The police are outside right now, ready to arrest me. They let me come in to use the bathroom. What am I going to do?"

CHAPTER SEVEN

Katie adjusted the phone to a more comfortable position. "You are going to do whatever the police tell you to do," she told Tiff. "And then we are going to get you a lawyer who can help you figure out what to do next."

"I have a lawyer," Tiff said. "Dad called the attorney who handles his estate, Mr. Morley, and he contacted a Mr. Leighton in Prescott."

"All right. When the police take you in, I believe you're entitled to one phone call. Use it to call Mr. Leighton and let him know what's going on."

Katie could hear a pounding on the door over the phone.

"I have to go," Tiff said.

The line went dead. It immediately rang again, before Katie could begin to think of what to do.

"I put the police off for a few more minutes." Tiff's voice was rushed. "Dad told me he sent Phil a letter.

He said Jeffrey had petitioned for guardianship, claiming Dad was no longer able to handle his own affairs. Dad married his caregiver, Lila, thinking that would eliminate any need for guardianship. Phil didn't show me the letter when he got it, but he said it sounded as if everyone was after Dad's money, which was why he wanted us to visit Dad right away. Dad kept a copy of the letter and said he also sent a copy to Mr. Morley, his attorney. I talked to his attorney. He said Dad hadn't been in touch with him for a while. He hadn't known about the marriage or about Jeffrey's actions. He said he would handle it now." Her voice suddenly raised to a shout. "I'm coming! Don't break the door down!" The line disconnected.

Wow, Katie thought. Is this the airheaded girl who didn't seem to care much about what had happened? But, there was nothing Katie could do. Mr. Leighton was the only one who could help Tiff at this point.

Since her grandmother was still asleep, Katie decided she could risk a quick trip back to the rental to shower in comfort and change into clothes for this afternoon. Nana hadn't awakened by the time Katie returned, so she busied herself with eliminating more of the clutter from the house until it was time to wake her grandmother.

"We're going to see your lawyer and your doctor this afternoon," Katie said when Nana, with very little help, was bathed and dressed.

"That's good," Nana said. "Then we'll know what I've done."

Katie looked at her in surprise. This was a different

person from the one last night. Her eyes were attentive, her movements slow but steady. She still didn't have much appetite, though. With a lot of coaxing, Nana downed a soft-boiled egg with half a piece of toast and a few sips of orange juice.

"Would you like to see my vacation rental?" Katie asked when they had finished. "And maybe stop somewhere for lunch?"

"That sounds like fun. I hope I don't get too tired."

"I'll make sure we don't do more than you are comfortable with," Katie said.

When they arrived at the rental, Tiff was there, her hair wet from showering. She looked wan and pale.

"How are you here and not in jail?" Katie asked.

Nana's head came up, her eyes bright with interest.

"Mr. Leighton came to the police station and demanded my release. He said they needed to do an initial appearance before they could hold me, and for that they needed some evidence. Chief Browning told him about the bag of poison, but Mr. Leighton insisted that unless my fingerprints were on it, because of the time lapse and second search before they found it, it was not grounds for arrest. That lawyer is really good. Chief Browning didn't have a chance against him."

"What are you going to do now?"

"I have an appointment with Mr. Leighton, but, I don't know what I can tell him. I don't understand about that weed, monkshood I think they called it, being found in the car. Phil and I went directly to the motel from the café. We never went back to the car. How did it get there?"

"That is a puzzle," Katie said. Which is probably why the chief decided you put it there, she thought. "But your car was at the motel while we were driving around. Anyone could have planted it."

———————

As soon as the door closed when they left the rental, Nana turned to Katie. "What was your friend in jail for?" she asked.

"Her husband was murdered and she's the main suspect."

"Did she say something happened at the café?"

"Yes. He was apparently poisoned by something in the salad he ate."

"Did she eat salad too?"

"Yes, but she didn't get sick." Katie stopped and turned to look at her grandmother. "No one else got sick, so it was only in his salad. That's why the police decided it was put there deliberately and Tiff was the only one who could have done it." She paused for a moment. "How would you like to have lunch at the ZigZag Café today?"

"I'd love it," Nana said, her eyes sparkling. "As long as we don't have a salad."

Katie looked at Nana in wonder. She'd have a hard time convincing anyone the grandmother she had with her today would have any problem taking care of herself. And she didn't care. She'd rather have this Nana.

Who could it have been, if not Tiff? Katie wondered as they entered the small restaurant. Something stubborn in her was reluctant to give up on Tiff just yet. If there was another explanation, no one would find it if they weren't looking for it. Oh, no! That must be how Mom got involved in police investigations.

The café was warm and inviting. Even though Phil's experience had to be a one-time thing, Katie still felt more comfortable joining Nana in a small soup and garlic bread rather than a salad. After they ordered, Katie asked the waitress, "Were you on duty the night of that unfortunate incident?'

The girl shuddered and looked around as if to be sure they weren't being observed. "No, I do breakfast and lunch, not dinner. But we've been told not to discuss it."

"I understand. That was my friend's husband, and I'm trying to find out what happened. If you know who was on duty that evening, I'd appreciate an opportunity to talk with her."

The girl visibly bristled. "Him," she said.

"Oh, dear," Nana intercepted. "Forgive my granddaughter. She finds it difficult to say 'him or her.'"

The girl relaxed, smiling at Nana. "I'll see what I can do," she said.

"Thank you, Nana," Katie said when the girl had gone to place their orders.

"And to think you were ready to put me away in an old folks' home."

Katie shrank back, stunned. "Nana, you are completely different now than you were last night," she said. "How do I know if this, the real you, is going to be in control tomorrow?"

"You don't. And neither do I. I hope we can figure out a solution to that problem together."

"So do I, Nana. So do I."

Their server returned with their soup and bread and put a slip of paper on the table. "His name is Greg Larson. He only works dinners. I think he goes to school in the daytime."

"Thank you so much," Katie said.

She left a generous tip when they had finished their lunch.

Nana seemed to be fading, so Katie took her home for an hour's rest before they went to Mrs. Andrews' office.

———

"Mrs. Andrews is running late," the receptionist told them when they arrived.

Katie had to hold back an angry comment when Mrs. Andrews, a tall, stout woman with steel-gray hair, who made Katie think of a stern school principal, strode in a good half an hour late. Nana did not need this.

The woman motioned for them to follow her into her office, and slapped a folder on her desk. "Now, what was it we needed to discuss?" she asked.

Katie took a deep breath to calm herself. "My grandmother is having difficulty remembering what arrangements Grandfather made before he died. She thinks you handled their affairs and would have a record of it."

Opening the folder, Mrs. Andrews said, "Mr. Christensen set up a trust, with Mrs. Christensen as trustee. He made arrangements for his pension payments and social security to be directly deposited into her bank account so she didn't have to worry about it on a day-to-day basis. That's probably why she doesn't remember what they did." She flipped through a few more pages. "There is also a 401(k), from which required minimum distributions are taken every month and also deposited into her checking account. To my knowledge, nothing more has been done."

"Did he make any provision for after Grandmother dies—or has she done so?"

"Robert Christensen is listed as successor trustee for your grandfather, followed by you, Ms. Christensen, in case Robert was unable or unwilling to take the responsibility. Since your grandfather left everything to your grandmother, the estate now belongs to her, and she has not updated it. Your grandfather did leave a message shortly before he died, indicating he might want to make an addendum to the trust. I don't know if he ever did that."

Nana looked confused. "I don't think anything has been done since my husband died, but everything will eventually go to Robert and Katherine, of course."

"Well, you probably don't need to do anything for that to happen, but I think we might want to put something in writing, anyway."

Katie glanced at Nana, but she had to ask the next question even if it upset her grandmother. "What happens if Nana is no longer able to handle her affairs? Has she set up a power of attorney and a healthcare directive?" Katie asked.

"To my knowledge, your grandmother has done neither of those. I'll have the papers drawn up and we can meet again to finalize them." She turned to Nana. "Who would you like to name as the person to handle your affairs if you are no longer able to do it?"

"Why, Robert, I suppose, since he's the oldest."

"But not here," Katie reminded her. "I am here to stay."

Nana looked confused.

"What would your brother have to say about it?" Mrs. Andrews asked.

"We talked yesterday and he indicated that since I am here I should probably be the one to take care of our grandmother."

Nana still looked confused, her eyes no longer sharp. "I don't know Kate. He is the oldest."

"All right, I believe your grandmother stated her preference. I am going to prepare a document giving your brother, Robert, the power of attorney if your grandmother can't handle her affairs. It'll name you second if he is unwilling or unable to perform the duties, which means he can turn the responsibility over to you at that time. However, I do think you should be the one named for handling healthcare issues since you are here. If that suits your grandmother, she can sign the documents when they are ready. Will that be all right?" Mrs. Andrews asked Nana.

"Yes, I guess so."

"I'm afraid I have another appointment now, but I'll get my staff working on this and give you a call when the papers are ready."

After talking her into eating most of a small ice cream cone, Katie took Nana home so she could lie down until they were due for her doctor's appointment.

———————

They were ushered into the examination room and Dr. Pelson arrived promptly. "I don't see any lasting damage," he said after checking Nana over. "What made you fall, Mrs. Christensen? Did you trip?"

"I don't think so. All I remember is being on the floor. When the phone rang, I could barely reach the cord to pull it down and was so relieved to hear Kate's voice."

"That you don't remember falling is a concern," Dr. Pelson said. "Of course, you and your granddaughter need to identify and remove anything that might cause you to trip, but we also need to check for other possible reasons for the fall."

"Doctor," Katie said, "yesterday I was really worried about my grandmother. She hardly ate anything, which I think has been going on for a while, and she was groggy and not coherent. Today she is much better, though she goes up and down a bit. Do you think the fall caused her problems yesterday?"

"Possibly. If she isn't eating properly, that could also contribute to it." He pinched the skin on top of Nana's hand. "She appears to be dehydrated, and she's definitely not quite up to par right now. Let's start with some blood work. I'd also like you to get a CT scan immediately, to rule out any other problems from the fall. Unless something turns up in the scan, I'll see you again in two weeks, when we have the blood work results."

After scheduling the follow-up appointment, they went a few doors down in the clinic for the CT scan. By the time they returned to Nana's house, she was fading fast.

"I'm perfectly all right, Kate ... Katie ..." Nana said after Katie had made sure she took a few bites of dinner and plied her with water. "You go back to your own place. I know not to eat anything in the morning and I don't get hungry, anyway, so you don't have to rush to take me for the blood draw."

"All right," Katie said. "Remember, the doctor said to drink a lot of water."

Nana managed a weak laugh. "How many times do you think I want to get up tonight?"

Katie hoped Nana really would be all right, because she wanted to find out what was going on with Tiff.

As she approached the rental, she saw two police cars blocking the driveway. *Now what?* Heart pounding, she parked on the street and walked with a restrained stride to the rental.

"What's going on?" she asked the first policeman she encountered.

"We're here to arrest Tiffany Wells." He looked almost sorry to tell her.

Struggling to keep her voice from reflecting her growing agitation, Katie said, "Yes, but you arrested her earlier and let her go. What is going on now?"

He didn't have a chance to respond before Tiff emerged, eyes puffy from crying, escorted by a policewoman.

"Tiff, what is happening?" Katie asked.

"It's Dad," Tiff cried. "He's dead. He's been murdered too. And they think I did it."

"Why do they think you did it?" Katie called as a policewoman put Tiff into one of the police cars. Tiff didn't have a chance to answer. Katie's last sight of Tiff was a pale face with stringy hair and round, frightened eyes staring a plea out the window.

CHAPTER EIGHT

Katie whirled on the officer. "Why do you think she did it?"

"I'm not at liberty to speak to you about the case."

"Right. Don't talk about it and you might get her convicted without a fight? Not going to happen," she snapped and headed toward her rental.

"Wait right there," the detective said.

"Why? Do you have a search warrant?"

He looked uncertain. Chief Browning emerged from the rental unit, giving Katie a crooked grin. "We're finished here," he said. He and the detective piled into the second police car and drove away. Katie stared after them. The air suddenly felt empty. She hesitated to go in, feeling violated even before looking at what havoc they might have caused. Again. She took a deep breath and entered.

It wasn't as bad as she had feared. Things were moved about a bit but not like a real search. It was almost as if they didn't expect to find anything; or perhaps they no longer had a valid search warrant. Whichever it was, Katie would bet the chief was doing everything he could to annoy her.

Locating Mr. Leighton's number, Katie called to let him know Tiff was back in custody for her father-in-law's murder.

"Do you know what evidence they have?" the attorney asked.

"No, the police were taking Tiff away when I arrived at the rental and they wouldn't tell me anything."

"All right, I'll take it from here. Thanks for calling me."

"Please let me know what you find out. I've somehow become Tiff's only friend and I'd like to help her if I can."

"Will do," he said and disconnected.

Katie worried her lower lip with her teeth after hanging up. She had no reason to believe Tiff didn't kill both her husband and her father-in-law. She sighed, shaking her head. Guilty or not, the girl needed a friend. It appeared the God Mom always said had a hand in things had selected her for that purpose.

She wanted nothing more than to fall into bed and sleep until she had to take Nana for her blood work in the morning, but she couldn't do that yet. Greg Larson, the server who had been on duty the night Phil was poisoned, was working at the café tonight. Tiff's attorney should probably be the one to talk with him, but he was busy looking after Tiff right now. If Greg had any information that could help, Katie would let Mr. Leighton know.

The dinner hour was winding down when she arrived. Greg told her he'd meet her at the Top View Bar and Grill when his shift finished in an hour.

The Top View Bar was well named. It sat on a level piece of ground high on a hill about half a mile north of Cactus City. Driving into the parking lot, Katie could see that it had a view from its deck across a deep valley to the distant mountains.

She parked the Maserati and took a few breaths of the already cooling air to release the day's tensions before walking into the dimly lit room. Soft music filled the air. The only television, tuned to a sports station, was in a separate room, where its noise was less disturbing than in most bars.

A sudden roar from that room made Katie look up at the waitress who had arrived at her table.

"Not from around here?" the waitress asked with a toothy smile that made Katie like her immediately.

"No, arrived a couple days ago," Katie said.

"The Diamondbacks just got a home run," the waitress said.

"Not against the Mariners, I hope," Katie said.

The waitress laughed and held out her hand. "You must be from Seattle, but not a Mariners fan or you'd know their schedule. No, against the Texas Rangers this time. Our Diamondbacks are on a roll this year. My name is Marta. My brother owns this place."

"I'm Katie. I like what he's done with it. It's hard to enjoy a drink when you have to listen to at least four

TVs blaring four different events at the same time in the same room."

"Exactly. Of course, we get some complaints when people can't watch the event they want. I tell them to go on into town to the Low-End Bar to do that. We get plenty of business the way it is."

"Good for you," Katie said. "I'll have a double shot of bourbon on the rocks with a glass of water on the side."

"You've got it," Marta said. Katie admired the woman's softly rounded features and wavy, shoulder-length, brown hair as she walked over to the bar to give the order. When she returned, she asked, "You alone?"

"Greg, from the ZigZag Café, will be joining me in a few minutes." Marta looked a little surprised. Katie thought she saw a trace of disapproval in the girl's brown eyes. "I need to talk with him about something that happened in the café," she hastened to add, so Marta wouldn't get the wrong idea. Greg was, after all, a few years younger than Katie; closer to Marta's age. "Do you know Greg?"

Marta retrieved Katie's drink. "We went to high school together. He was my date for the senior prom. Now he's more like my brother than someone I'd date. I assume you are talking about that man who got poisoned."

"Yes."

Katie could see the curiosity in Marta's eyes, but she didn't feel comfortable talking to a stranger about Tiff's situation. She was spared the need to elaborate by Greg striding across the room. Marta went to the bar and returned with a beer the bartender had ready before Greg reached the table.

"The dinner crowd thinned out," he explained, sitting across from Katie. "So, they let me go early. They know I have to study for an exam tomorrow. How can I help you?"

"You served the salads to the man who died, and his wife?"

He stiffened. "Yes?"

Katie smiled. "No one suspects you of anything. The police believe his wife poisoned him with that salad, so they aren't looking into other possibilities. I'm not so sure, so I'd like to know if anything unusual happened while you were serving them."

"Unusual, like what?"

"Did you see anyone in or near the kitchen who didn't belong there?"

"No. But if that's where the poison was put in the salad, how would the person know which one of them would get that salad—or even be sure those salads were going to that table?"

Katie considered. "Maybe it didn't matter which one died," she mused. "Did anything happen to distract your attention while you were taking the salads to the table?"

"No ... wait, yes. Someone bumped into me, almost knocking them out of my hands." He paused. "And it must have been pretty obvious by then which table would get them."

"Can you describe the person?" Katie asked, excitement rising.

"No, it happened too fast and I was busy holding onto the plates. But, even if he could put something in the salad, how would he know which salad was going to the man?"

"Maybe the way you were approaching the table?"

Greg seemed to consider this. "Yes, I was going straight to the table with her on my right and him on my left. Since we serve ladies first and from the left, he could be pretty sure the one in my right hand would go to her and I'd walk around the table to serve him."

"Which side was the person on when he bumped into you?"

"The left."

"Did you see where he went after he bumped you?"

"Straight out the door. I figured that was where he was headed and he hadn't been watching where he was going. He was wearing a hoodie, but the hood was hanging down his back and he had a cap pulled down over his eyes, which is not unusual in this area."

Katie's cell phone rang. She glanced at the display. "I'm sorry, I have to take this," she said. "But I still have a quick question. Hello, Mr. Leighton? Could you hold for a moment?" She turned back to Greg. "I hope you are willing to talk to Tiff's attorney about this." At Greg's nod, she went back to the phone and told Mr. Leighton what she had learned.

While she was on the phone, Greg slipped a piece of paper over the table to her and mouthed "Have to go study." Katie glanced at it to see it contained his contact information so she read it to the attorney before they continued their conversation.

"Can you tell me anything about the charges against Tiff?" she asked the attorney, taking a small sip of her drink.

"Yes. Unfortunately, Mr. Wells' wife, Lila, says she found him dead when she returned home from shopping sometime after Tiffany left. The Phoenix police determined that he had been smothered. The house showed signs of a break-in and burglary, and when the police caught up with Tiffany in Cactus City and searched her car, several of the stolen items were found."

"Really!" Katie exploded. "This makes no sense at all. Why would Tiff have to break in when she had a perfectly legitimate reason to be there? To make it look like a burglary? But would she be stupid enough to keep the missing items in her car?"

"Apparently, that's what they think," Mr. Leighton said. "Lila Wells claims Jim Wells didn't agree to see Tiffany, so she must have broken in and killed him when she couldn't get whatever she wanted. The Phoenix police seem to think she was going to dispose of the items but they got to her before she could. They do have her fingerprints in his house."

"Of course, her fingerprints were in his house. She went to visit him." Katie took a deep breath, reviewing what the attorney had said. "So, some of the missing items were in her car. But not all of them?"

"The police can't be sure. They had Jeffrey take a

look, since they weren't comfortable relying solely on Mrs. Wells' word. He said he thought more things were missing, but he couldn't be positive Mr. Wells hadn't disposed of them earlier."

"Where was Jeffrey when the murder happened?"

"I don't know. The police seem to think he has an alibi that they weren't willing to share with me, but I'll be checking into it."

"Does Tiff have any idea when the stolen items could have been put into her car?"

"She says she wasn't feeling well while she was driving back up Route 17 so she stopped at Sunset Point Scenic View and walked around for a while. She says she didn't bother to lock her car since she wasn't going to be there long. I managed to find out that there were no fingerprints on the items in her car."

"None? Yet she left fingerprints in the house? I wonder if they found any gloves. Anyway, leaving the car open made it easy for someone who was following her to quickly put a few things in her car."

"Exactly. But, of course, we have no way to prove it."

Katie took a deep breath. "I don't think Tiff is stupid enough to keep things stolen from her father-in-law in her car. If she planned to dispose of them, she could easily have done that at Sunset View or any-where along the way. Now I am more convinced than ever that Tiff is being set up. I can't think of anyone besides Jeffrey who would have a motive to do it, but I have no idea how Mr. Wells' recent marriage might figure in."

Katie continued to nurse her drink after disconnecting, trying to sort through what she had learned. She was grateful Tiff had an attorney who had her best interests in mind and who seemed to be on the right track.

She drummed her fingers on the table. Tiff had no alibi for either murder. In fact, she seemed to be the only person present at the time both murders occurred. If she had no way to prove she didn't do them, the only chance to prove her innocence was to discover who really did.

CHAPTER NINE

Jeffrey had been trying to gain control of his uncle's estate before all this happened. Mr. Wells evidently thwarted his nephew's plans by taking a new wife, Lila. Who knew what this new wife was up to? Even if both Jeffrey and Lila had solid alibis for the murders, either one could have hired someone else to do the deeds.

But, how would they have known when and where Phil and Tiff were going to stop for dinner? How could anyone have known?

Tiff apparently decided to visit Mr. Wells after Katie had gone out this morning. She must have called to tell Mr. Wells she was coming. Had Lila Wells or someone else overheard that conversation and made a plan to incriminate Tiff? While Jeffrey and Lila said the things in Tiff's car belonged to Mr. Wells, Jeffrey thought other things might be missing too. Why would Tiff have some of the stolen items, but not all of them?

Katie didn't know how to answer those questions. Nor did she know how much Lila stood to gain from her husband's death. She shook her head. Maybe Mr. Morley would have some ideas about what else was going on in Jim Wells' life, but she'd have to wait until tomorrow to get in touch with him.

This was getting her nowhere and she needed sleep. Dropping money for her tab and a tip on the table, she stood to leave. She eyed her glass, which was still almost half full of her now very diluted drink. She resisted the urge to pick it up and finish it.

Approaching the rental, Katie peered toward the door and slowed down. Was it a trick of the shadows or was someone trying to get in?

She drove past and stopped around a bend, where the light from opening the car door wouldn't alert the trespasser to her presence. Stepping out, she eased the door as far shut as she could without making any noise. Creeping back to the driveway, she could see she was right. Someone with a lumpy bag on the ground was trying to get in. Pulling out her cell phone, she dialed 911. The dispatcher's response was remarkably loud in the quiet night. The intruder's head jerked up.

Running forward, Katie shouted into the phone, "Someone is breaking into my rental!" Dogs on this side of the unit started barking. Instantly out of breath, she managed to gasp out the address while she stopped, picked up a rock, and threw it at the intruder's arm as he reached to pick up the bag. The intruder pulled back, hesitated, and reached out again. Katie was ready with a larger rock. She always had good aim, and this one hit the intruder's wrist with an audible whack. The intruder cried out, turned, and staggered away, grasping his wrist. By now, dogs on that side were also barking. Katie tried to take up the chase, at least to see which way the intruder went in case the police arrived quickly, but she had to stop at the doorstep, panting.

"Will I ever get used to this altitude?" she muttered as she slumped down onto the step to wait for the police.

"So, what did he look like?" Chief Browning barked. He sounded as if he thought she had made the whole thing up. He can't deny the fresh scrapes on the keyhole, though, Katie thought.

"It was too dark for me to make out any features, but the person was wearing a hoodie and a cap, like the one in the café."

"How do you know anything about a person in the café?"

"I talked to the waiter who served Phil and Tiff their salads, and he told me about a man in a hoodie and a cap. Didn't you talk with him?"

The chief scowled. Katie wondered if he hadn't bothered, or if he hadn't asked the right questions. He obviously thought he had the case all figured out.

The bag proved to contain items Katie suspected were the rest of the missing ones from Jim Wells' house. She frowned in puzzlement. "It looks as if someone was planting more evidence against Tiff. Perhaps the thief planned on keeping these items but, since Jeffrey identified them, thought he needed to put them in her possession. But didn't you already search when you picked her up?" She paused, shaking her head. "I don't know. Maybe he thought he could find a place you wouldn't have thought to look. But, you have to admit, this shows someone is trying to frame her."

"We looked around, of course, but couldn't do a real search because we needed a new search warrant for that. Of course, you could have done this whole thing yourself to take suspicion off of her," the chief drawled.

"You won't find any instrument capable of making those marks on the doorknob anywhere near me, unless the intruder dropped it, and, even if he did, you won't find my fingerprints on it," Katie retorted. "Besides, where would I have gotten that bag of stuff?"

"From your friend Tiffany Wells."

Katie heard the uncertainty in his voice. "So, for some reason I'm trying to break into my own place, for which I have a key, with a bag of stolen goods I somehow got from Tiff, who I only saw while she was being arrested. Why would I want to put stolen goods where I live? And why would I call 911?"

The chief threw up his hands and started to walk away.

"I'm calling Tiff's attorney with this information. I'm betting it will throw enough doubt on Tiff's guilt that you won't be able to hold her for the Phoenix police."

"Give it your best shot!" he shouted over his shoulder. Katie was sure it was all bravado now.

To Katie's relief, Mr. Leighton answered his phone despite the late hour. "I'll be able to use this tomorrow," he said when she had relayed the information to him. "They are holding Tiffany overnight, but I will be objecting to this since she has not had an initial appearance. If necessary, I'll take her to Phoenix for that in the morning."

He paused. Katie could almost hear the gears turning in his head. "I'm sure the events at your rental will throw enough doubt on that charge to prevent her arraignment at this time. I believe Chief Browning has also realized he doesn't have good enough evidence to proceed with the initial appearance for her husband's murder. So, we will be at a standstill unless either of them finds some additional evidence."

"Thank you, Mr. Leighton. You have given me reason to believe we can put this behind us. But I hope we can prove Tiff isn't guilty of either murder, not just leave it in limbo."

Katie had planned to make an overdue call to her mother tonight, but when she was finally free to do so, she collapsed on the bed and was asleep before she could change her clothes.

She awoke with a start and looked at the clock. Eight thirty. She hadn't intended to sleep so late. Nana needed to go for her fasting blood test. After a quick shower, with still wet hair, which meant she would soon have a mass of unruly curls around her head, Katie took off for Nana's. As promised, Nana had not eaten, but she also was not out of bed, showered, or in any way ready to go. Katie had to bite her tongue to keep from hurrying Nana along.

They finally got to the lab where Nana had her blood samples taken. Katie took a deep breath as they left. "Now, do you want to get breakfast somewhere?"

"Didn't we eat at the café yesterday?"

"Well, yes, but we could do it again, since we're already out," Katie replied. She needed to remember that in Nana's day, going out to eat only happened on special occasions.

"Oh, but since you bought groceries yesterday, I think we need to eat at home. We don't want them to go to waste."

Katie didn't think anything she had purchased would spoil in a day or three or a week, but she smiled and took her grandmother home.

Nana actually ate a fair amount of the scrambled eggs and half a slice of the toast Katie prepared. Maybe all it required was having someone around who would make Nana take better care of herself.

Katie's cell phone rang while she was washing the dishes. "Mr. Leighton," she said. "I hope you have good news for me."

"I do," he said. "As you know, I took Tiffany down for an initial appearance at court in Phoenix this morning. The Phoenix police didn't want Tiffany to be released, claiming the investigation wasn't complete and she was a flight risk. Fortunately, the judge determined that they couldn't hold someone on insufficient evidence even if they thought she was a flight risk." He paused. "That's the good news. Unless something more happens in the Cactus City case, I don't believe the police can restrict her movements there, either. Staying in Cactus City may help her case, though, should she be charged. Anyway, we're on our way back now, and I'll take her directly to your place."

"I'll meet you there," she said, disconnecting. "Nana, do you want to go to my rental?"

"Goodness, no. I've gone out more since you've been here than I have in years. You'll have me plumb worn out."

"I doubt that," Katie said with a laugh. "But we have plenty of time for lunch right here before I go. You have sandwich makings, soup, and cottage cheese, among other things."

"Oh, don't fuss. Besides, didn't we just finish breakfast a few minutes ago?"

Katie chuckled again. She was getting rattled with so much going on, rushing ahead without thinking about what she was doing. That wasn't good. And, anyway, Tiff wouldn't be home for an hour and a half or so.

Declaring it her nap time, Nana retreated to her bedroom. Unable to sit still, Katie spent the time filling a box with throw rugs to take to a thrift shop and removing unnecessary obstacles to walking in the small space.

"What are you doing with my things?" Nana asked in a querulous voice when she reappeared from her bedroom after a short nap.

"Dr. Pelson said we need to fall-proof your house. If you have a special attachment to any of these things, we'll try to find a place to put them where they don't create a risk."

Nana looked over the items Katie had put aside, a frown on her face. "No special attachment," she finally admitted. "They are just the things that made my house feel like home."

Katie swallowed hard. This was not going to be easy. Before she had to decide what to remove and what to keep, Katie's phone rang. It was Mr. Leighton, informing her that he and Tiff were in Cactus City. She hugged Nana, reminded her to eat, and raced out of the house.

———————

Mr. Leighton and Tiff were leaning against the car waiting for Katie when she arrived. "A night in jail!" Katie exclaimed as she jumped out of the Maserati. "What was that like? Why are you waiting out here?"

Tiff gave a weak laugh. "Not my first choice of how to spend a night in the mountains. I was so confused about what was going on last night, I didn't think to grab my key." She burst into tears.

"Paul Leighton," the attorney said, shaking Katie's hand. The two of them guided Tiff into the rental.

"Is this a reaction to your day, or is there some other reason for the tears?" Katie asked when they were seated around the dining room table.

"A little bit of both," Tiff said, drying her eyes. "If I'm understanding everything, Jeffrey may have murdered both Phil and Dad, hoping to pin it on me so I couldn't inherit." Tiff took a deep breath. She looked as if she were holding back a fresh onslaught of tears.

"Well, when I went to Phoenix, Dad's wife wasn't there. Dad was so nice; he didn't blame me for what happened to Phil at all. He said I should move in with them. He didn't want me to be on my own because …" Now the tears came again. "Because I'm pregnant."

Katie stared at the attorney. "So, if someone is trying to set Tiff up for the murders so she can't get the money, they'll be disappointed. Even if she were somehow convicted of murdering both Phil and Jim, according to the trust document we know about, Phil's child will benefit before anyone else."

"Mr. Wells' marriage might change everything," said Mr. Leighton. "However, if Mr. Wells made provision for Phil and Tiff, and if Jeffrey or Lila is trying to get their hands on it, this will definitely throw a monkey wrench into their plans."

"But what will they do?" Tiff wailed. "Will they try to get rid of the baby? Will they find a way to blame that on me too?"

Katie shook her head. Now she knew she had to help sort this out. She remembered her mom saying things always went wrong when you took the easy solution without examining all of the possibilities. As little as Katie knew about Phil and his father, or Lila, Tiff, and Jeffrey, for that matter, she had no idea what possibilities to start examining. Given that, she should probably leave it to the professionals.

The problem was, the professionals seemed convinced they had their culprit—Tiff—so they might not look any further. They seemed to have ruled out Jeffrey because they had verified his alibis. The only other possibility Katie could see was the new wife, Lila. What could Katie do to find out about her?

She turned back to Tiff's attorney. "Mr. Leighton, I don't suppose there is any way we could get into Jim Wells' house to see what we can discover?"

Mr. Leighton shook his head. "That would surely require permission from his wife. Whether or not she ends up with the house, it is her home right now. I'm also sure Mr. Morley will take whatever steps are necessary to settle Mr. Wells' affairs. What would you hope to find?"

"I don't know. My mother has been involved in several murder investigations, and she often succeeds where the police don't because she will leave no stone unturned. I'm trying to find stones to turn." She looked at Tiff, who had been quietly crying throughout this exchange. Phil's death certainly upset her life, but his father's death complicated things even more. "Are you still planning to move from San Diego?"

"I don't know what I'm going to do, but I have no reason to stay there. I have no brothers or sisters. My mother died several years ago, and my father is remarried to a woman who wants me out of his life." Tears surfaced again. "Phil's dad was the only person who cared about me, even after Phil was killed." Her voice took on a dreamy quality. "It would have been so great to live with him."

Katie shook off a feeling of impatience. That was obviously what Tiff had been relying on, but it was time for her to grow up and start taking care of herself. "Did you finish any of the things we talked about before you took off for Phoenix?"

Tiff shook her head. "I thought Dad would help me. And he was going to before ..." her voice trailed off.

"You need to find out what details of your life have to be dealt with right away," Katie said before Tiff could dissolve into tears again. "Since you can't go to San Diego right now, is there someone you could ask to send you any important papers?"

"My friend Judith, but I wouldn't know what to tell her to look for."

Katie tapped a finger on the table while she thought. "If you don't plan to go back to San Diego, she could send you everything except obvious trash."

"Well, I'm not going back to that apartment. I couldn't stand to be there without Phil. And I have no reason to stay in San Diego, so, I might as well get everything out of there now."

"Why don't you ask your friend if she can help you do that? In addition to getting the paperwork required to take care of your affairs now, we need to see if we can figure out what might have been going on in Phil's life, or his father's, that would put them both in this kind of jeopardy."

Tiff got on her cell to call Judith and ask her to handle things at that end. While they were talking, Mr. Leighton called Mr. Morley's office to see if Mr. Morley needed any more information from Tiff.

Tiff disconnected and turned to Katie. "I asked Judith to box up all of the papers except junk mail and send them here. When I told her why, she said deciding what was important would be too hard, mailing them would take too long, and overnighting them would be expensive. She wants to see me, anyway, so she is going to bring every scrap of paper to us."

"Mr. Morley says he needs to get into Mr. Wells' papers in his home office to see what he has done since he set up his original trust," Mr. Leighton said. "He'll set up a meeting to explain the trust provisions and any other formalities as soon as he's sure he has the most current information. Since we don't know what arrangements Mr. Wells made before or after marrying, we don't know who will get possession of the house."

Tiff turned to Katie, her blue eyes as round as saucers. "Wow. I might own a house? If I do, will you stay in my house with me? It's big!"

Katie couldn't help but grin. The innocent, naïve Tiff kept popping up at the moment when Katie was beginning to doubt her existence. "Don't count on it," she said. "Normally the house goes to the wife. Anyway, I can't abandon Nana in Cactus City." She turned back to Mr. Leighton. "I hope Mr. Morley also finds clues that would tell us if Mr. Wells was up to something that might have led to his murder."

Tiff put a hand over her mouth to stifle a giggle. "I'm sorry," she said, "it's just, you know, the idea of Dad being 'up to' anything is so weird. He was such a straight arrow." Tears pooled again, ready to spill over.

Mr. Leighton cleared his throat. "If your friend arrives with your papers tomorrow or the next day, I expect you to contact me immediately so I can make sure anything of interest is handled properly."

"Of course," Tiff said, ushering the attorney to the door.

"It has to be Jeffrey," she said, whirling on Katie as soon as the door was closed. "Why aren't you helping me get evidence against him instead of muddying the waters with all this other stuff?"

"No, it doesn't have to be Jeffrey." Katie tried to keep impatience out of her voice. "One could as easily say it has to be you, or Lila. I certainly hope the police or your attorney are trying to find out if Jeffrey's alibis stand up, because I don't know how we would do that, but let's look at everything and make sure we have ruled out all other possibilities before making an accusation."

Tiff pouted but, being in Katie's living room, she had no place to go to nurse her pique in private. Katie took pity on her and retreated to the bedroom to give the girl some space.

It was way past time to call Mom. She dialed her mother's cell number, but the call went to voicemail.

Why wouldn't she answer? She kept her cell phone with her and she always answered. Was she in the hospital or someplace where she couldn't answer her phone? Had something happened to Benjamin or Eric?

Katie couldn't believe how much the thought of that possibility upset her. "Call me back," she said, "no matter what time it is."

After hanging up she realized her mother could be in any number of places where she couldn't answer the phone. She also could easily interpret Katie's words as an emergency in Katie's life rather than Katie wanting to know what was going on with her. Well, so be it. Worry would make her more likely to call back immediately.

Katie laid back on her bed, trying to focus her thoughts. Everything was so up in the air. She had to figure out what to do about Nana. What about her own life? She needed a job and a permanent place to live.

And how did that compare to Tiff's position: the loss of a husband and father-in-law, the possible arrest for the murder of both, and the discovery that she was pregnant? Katie's anxiety level shot up every time she thought about Tiff being pregnant. If Tiff was innocent, and Katie was more and more convinced she was, and the real culprits found out she was pregnant, what might that mean?

CHAPTER TEN

At midnight, Katie's cell phone jarred her out of a sound sleep.

"I'm sorry to call so late," her mother said, her voice anxious. "But you did say to call no matter how late it was. What is happening?"

Why did I do that? Katie wondered. She frowned in concentration as the fog gripping her brain started to clear. "Oh, I'm sorry, Mom. I hope I didn't frighten you. There is no emergency, though Nana isn't doing well. I asked you to call back immediately because I was afraid, when I couldn't reach you, that something might have happened to you or one of the boys."

"You were worried about the boys?"

Katie could almost hear her mother's smile. "Yeah, I really was," Katie admitted. "So, is everything okay with all of you?"

"Yes, it is. We were at a celebration dinner that went on quite late after a meeting with the adoption caseworkers. We have been approved to adopt both of the boys."

"Oh, Mom, congratulations! I know how much this means to you. So, now I have two little brothers to pick on?"

"Yes, yes you do. How soon do you plan to come home to do it?"

Katie sobered. "I have a couple of problems with that." She proceeded to tell her mother about the situation with Nana. "I can't leave until I know she has the oversight needed to keep her safe."

"Of course," Mom said. "And you are going to be faced with some difficult decisions to make sure of that. But, you said a couple of problems?"

Mom remained silent as Katie related everything that had happened since her arrival in Cactus City.

"I have no intention of taking up your mantle for crime solving," Katie finished. "But I can't see Tiff being railroaded for something she may not have done."

"But, you're not sure?" Mom said.

"Well, not totally positive. But pretty sure. The police chief here, in Cactus City, seems to be convinced she is guilty, so I need to help her attorney find out who is so bent on getting her accused of two murders, if she didn't do them."

"Keep digging, Kate. That is the only advice I can give you. Every time an angle opens up for you to explore, explore it. Even Pete will admit that sometimes the police put on blinders, following one trail and ignoring all the others. They need to solve cases.

And because they have a heavy load of cases, it is understandable if sometimes they take the easy way out."

Katie sighed. "That's sort of what I figured," she said. "Sure wish I knew where to dig next."

Mom laughed. "I have every confidence that your brilliant legal mind will come up with something."

"Well, I'll let you know in a day or two if I do."

After they said good-bye, Katie disconnected. Her mind drifted as she fell back on her bed. What was she going to do about Nana? How was she going to find a job? She flipped onto her side and tried to force her eyes closed.

They refused to stay shut, so she got up and tip-toed to the kitchen to brew a cup of chamomile tea. Taking it back to her room, she glanced at the tousled hair spilling out from under the blankets on the sofa-bed and frowned.

If the guilty person wasn't Tiff or Jeffrey, who could it be? Lila? If someone else had an interest in Jim Wells' estate, they would surely come out of the woodwork pretty soon. How large was the estate, anyway? It must be pretty big to tempt anyone to risk the charge of murder to acquire it.

Katie wondered how much they could find out from Mr. Wells' attorney. It might be a conflict of interest for him to help Tiff since she was suspected of killing his client. Unfortunately, Katie didn't think she would get a chance to look through Mr. Wells' papers. Mr. Morley would take charge of them. A conversation with Mr. Morley might answer a lot of questions—if he was open to her being involved. She hoped Mr. Leighton would help make that possible.

Despite the turmoil of her thoughts, Katie fell into a fitful sleep for the rest of the night.

Sleeping later than usual, Katie was awakened at nine by a banging on the door. She stumbled out of her room in time to see Tiff open the door and throw her arms around a short, round woman who looked to be in her early thirties, closer to Katie's age than Tiff's.

"How did you get here so fast?" Tiff asked.

"I couldn't sleep after you told me what had happened, so I threw all the papers together from your apartment and drove all night."

Tiff pulled the woman and the suitcase she was carrying into the room. "Katie, this is my good friend Judith. She has been so much help to me since we moved to San Diego. And, Judith, Katie rescued me when I needed it the most."

Katie eyed the suitcase. She appreciated what Judith was doing for Tiff, but there wasn't room in this small place for another person.

"I came here first, to give you this," Judith said, handing the suitcase to Tiff. "It's stuffed with every scrap of paper left in your apartment after I threw out the ads, solicitations, magazines, and other junk mail. Now, I'm going to go back to that motel at the edge of town and see if I can get a room to crash for a few hours. I'll talk to you this afternoon."

Tiff looked as if she was about to object, but Judith was gone before she could say anything.

"I'm going to start a pot of coffee and take a quick shower," Katie said. "You can begin sorting through that stuff if you want to, or wait until I can help you."

"Go ahead with your shower. I'll make the coffee. I might make a stab at this before you come out, but I need to freshen up, too, before I'll feel like doing any real work on it."

An hour later they were seated at the dining room table, Katie with her coffee and Tiff with a cup of tea and a slice of dry toast. They made one pass through the papers, discarding unnecessary receipts and other papers they determined would never be of any use. That left a stack of mail, mostly unopened, and several file folders—Phil's work papers in one; their apartment lease and related documents in another; three folders of tax materials, bank statements, and other financial information; and one with miscellaneous documents.

"Have you informed Phil's employer about his death?" Katie asked. At Tiff's downcast look, Katie found the phone number in Phil's work folder. Tiff made the call while Katie rifled through the rest of the folder.

"Phil has a small life insurance policy through his company that you'll need to apply for as soon as you have the death certificate," she said when Tiff disconnected. "Have you started a list of the things you need to do?"

"No, every time I tried to do anything I was being hauled down to the police station."

Katie found a writing pad and pen and handed them to Tiff. "Start now," she said.

Soon Tiff had written down giving a month's notice at her apartment, disposing of the belongings she didn't intend to keep, and changing joint bank information to her name. She sat back. "If I ever get cleared of murder charges, even if I get Dad's house, I don't want to live there. It would always be his house in my mind, and it's, like, really big. I don't know what to do."

Katie was looking through the remainder of the papers. "You have time for those decisions after we find out what you actually have and what you can do with it. You have a couple of bills here, and you have some unopened mail that must have arrived since you left. You should probably have your mail forwarded to a post office box in Cactus City until you get things sorted out. You can take care of that at the post office today."

Tiff took the stack of unopened envelopes, tossed a couple of pieces of junk mail, and added a couple more bills to the pile. When she reached the last envelope, she sat up and gasped.

"This is another letter to Phil from Dad," she cried. With shaking hands, she opened the envelope and read the single sheet of paper it contained.

"He did make an addendum to his trust," she said. "He did it quickly, without consulting Mr. Morley, so it would be done before anyone could stop him. But, he says it is all legal, witnessed, and notarized and everything, and he would get a copy to Mr. Morley as soon as possible. He says he made Phil and Jeffrey equal beneficiaries to accounts that contain about three million dollars, so they won't be named in the trust. I am secondary beneficiary to Phil's share, with any child Phil has next in line." She glanced up, her eyes huge, and mouthed a "Wow!" before going on. "He adds that he expects they will be more than satisfied with that. He left a million to Lila, and she agreed to that in a prenuptial agreement. The residue is to go to a foundation he recently learned about that provides educational grants to young people in need." She looked at Katie. "Residue? How much residue could there be?"

"Does he give the name of the foundation? Or the amount of the residue?"

"No. That's all he says."

"I'm going to send this to Mr. Leighton and Mr. Morley. Mr. Morley needs to check out that foundation."

Tiffany stared at her. "Why? Do you think something is wrong with it? It sounds like a good cause."

"Of course, it does. Otherwise Jim Wells wouldn't have left money to it. But unscrupulous groups have a way of preying on the elderly and using their good intentions to divert money to themselves." Katie paused in thought. "All right, you have a lot to do and I have to send this information, check on my grandmother, and start looking for an apartment."

Nana didn't answer her phone. Did that mean she wasn't functioning well again? Perhaps she was still asleep and didn't hear it. Whatever, it reawakened concerns about her living conditions. Maybe Katie should be trying to find a place big enough for both of them. If she did, would Nana agree to leave her little home and live with Katie?

CHAPTER ELEVEN

At the public library in Cactus City, Katie found e-mail addresses for both attorneys, scanned the letter, and sent a copy to each of them before hurrying to her grandmother's house.

Nana didn't answer her knock, so she let herself in with the key she had. There was no sign anyone had been in this part of the house since Katie left yesterday. Chest constricted with fear and worry, Katie went to the bedroom door. Nana was fast asleep, her breathing steady and normal as far as Katie could tell. She let out a huge sigh of relief. It was almost noon, though, so Nana should be out of bed and getting something to eat.

As Katie stroked Nana's shoulder, her eyes fluttered open, unfocused. "Nana? It's time to eat something. You should get up now."

"So, now you're going to tell me when to get out of bed? Have I lost the ability to decide for myself?"

Nana's voice was uncharacteristically sharp, making Katie step back. She wanted to say no, of course not; unfortunately, that was exactly what she had done. But her grandmother *should* be out of bed by noon, shouldn't she?

Katie went into the kitchen and started a pot of coffee. "Do you want eggs or cereal for breakfast?" she called out.

"I don't want breakfast," Nana said, her voice still querulous.

Katie took a deep breath. "Lunch? Soup? You need to eat something."

"I'm not hungry. Maybe a piece of toast and coffee."

As long as Nana was willing to eat something, Katie decided to wait her out and let her have her way. She had picked up a copy of the small *Cactus Weekly* at the library, so she poured herself a cup of coffee and sat down to read the apartment rental section. She circled three she thought might work and sat back, chewing her lip. She wanted to get a place big enough for Nana and her to live together, but she was certain Nana would not agree to that. She couldn't lock herself into a long-term lease, though, until she knew whether Nana could stay by herself or whether Katie would have to force the issue.

Nana emerged from the bedroom in her robe, her hair uncombed. She looked frailer than Katie had ever seen her. With a sinking feeling, Katie worried that she couldn't handle this. As forceful and decisive as she had always been in her work life, she could not force her grandmother to eat or move or in any way tell her what to do. Nana needed a professional care-giver who was used to bullying, if necessary, to get her charges to do what was best for them.

Katie should probably go ahead and find an apart-ment for herself alone.

"Toast and coffee coming up," Katie said, seating Nana at the table. "Can I get you anything else?"

"I can help myself to whatever I need," Nana said, but her voice had become more reasonable. "I know I get careless sometimes, but I have been taking care of myself just fine."

Katie wasn't about to disagree with her right now. She put the toast and coffee in front of Nana and sat across from her. "Well, I'm going to start looking for apartments today," she said. "Do you want to come with me?"

"No, you go ahead. I'll do my crossword and watch my programs today. You young people keep going all the time, but I don't have that kind of energy anymore."

Katie smiled, hoping that was all it was. Maybe Nana slept so long today because Katie had tired her out too much. She'd have to be careful not to do that.

"I still don't know why you want to live here, though. What kind of work can you find in a small town like this?"

Katie grinned. "Maybe you have something to do with my wanting to move here." Picking up the paper, she started making calls for appointments to see the apartments. She finished a few minutes later, feeling fortunate that she would be able to see them all this afternoon.

Four hours later, Katie had looked at the apartments and filled out three applications, leaving them with the landlords. The rents were so reasonable compared to what she'd been paying in Seattle she decided to get a two-bedroom, just in case she needed space for Nana. Of course, in Seattle she had a high-paying job and could afford luxury and a view. These three had neither, but they were all clean and everything appeared to be in good working order.

Making herself trust that Nana could take care of herself, Katie returned to the rental, where she found Tiff collapsed on the sofa. Her long blonde hair was lank and oily looking. Her face was drawn.

"Are you all right?" Katie asked.

"I think so. As all right as a pregnant woman can be," Tiff answered.

"Were you able to get any of your things sorted out?" Katie asked. She didn't know how to react to Tiff's malaise. She had never been pregnant.

"Yes. I contacted Mr. Leighton and he came and looked over the paperwork I had. He took some of it with him—tax and other financial files. He said it wasn't his area, but he would keep them secure and find an accountant to help me when the time comes." Tiffany took a deep breath and rushed on, ticking things off on her fingers as she did. "I now have a post office box so my mail can be forwarded here. I have prepared a written notice for leaving my apartment. I asked Judith to arrange for someone to pack up any personal things for shipping here and have the furnishings taken to a thrift store. That's where we got most of them anyway. She will also find a move-out cleaning service to make sure the apartment is in good condition. I can't do anything about the bank accounts until I have a death certificate for Phil, but since they are joint accounts, I still have access to them."

"Wow!" Katie said, thrown off by Tiff's shift from naïve innocence to efficient manager of her own affairs. "You accomplished a lot in one afternoon. So, is Judith on her way back to San Diego already?"

"She spent most of the day with me, and she'll stay the night at the motel and then head back tomorrow."

"She is doing so much for you. Should we at least take her out to dinner tonight in appreciation?"

Tiff grinned. "I hoped you'd like to join us for that. But I don't want to go to the ZigZag Café. I may never go in there again."

"How about if we take her to The Resort in Prescott? It's a little far, but I have seen some spectacular sunsets there when my grandparents took me. The food is good too."

"Sounds like a plan. I told her I'd pick her up at about four thirty, so I guess we'd better get moving."

An hour later, Tiff emerged from the bathroom, transformed. Black leggings with a light-blue-and-green design covered her long legs; topped by a long, loose, sleeveless green tunic. She wasn't showing signs of her pregnancy yet. With her hair washed and flowing over her shoulders, she looked like the California girl Katie had first met.

That left Katie about ten minutes to freshen up enough to face the evening.

Since Katie's Maserati was a two-seater, and Tiff had never driven the sharp, mountainous roads, Katie drove Tiff's car to Prescott. She breathed a sigh of relief when they reached The Resort an hour later. She didn't look forward to doing the switchbacks after dark when they returned, but she'd have to get used to driving them if she was going to live here. She would be going into Prescott Valley or Prescott for most of her shopping and nightlife.

The restaurant had the hushed feeling that Katie associated with fine dining. They settled at a table next to the large, west-facing window. Even before the sunset, the view was impressive, with Thumb Butte jutting into the sky as a centerpiece.

Since Katie was driving and Tiff was pregnant, they settled on tonic water with a twist for their drinks. Katie regretted being the driver. Living in Seattle she had never had to worry about drinking when she was out since she walked or took public transportation almost everywhere.

"It's too bad you can't stay a day or two and enjoy the mountains," Katie said to Judith after they ordered. Katie had selected a shrimp and clam spaghetti, Judith splurged on ribeye steak with garlic mashed potatoes, and Tiff settled for pasta with summer vegetables.

"Unfortunately, I have to get back to work the day after tomorrow, so I'll be leaving in the morning. I asked Tiff to make a list of the things we talked about today so I don't forget anything. Do you have it, Tiff?"

Tiff pulled a sheet of paper out of her pocket and unfolded it. Judith took a pen from her purse and looked it over.

"I hope it's not too much to ask," Tiff said. "I'd take care of most of it myself if I could leave town. I don't think old butthead would like that, though."

Judith began reading the list aloud. "Hand your notice to the apartment manager. That's easy. I'll do that as soon as I get back. Are you going to lose your deposit?"

"Maybe. We weren't there a year yet. But it wouldn't hurt to remind them of the circumstances, if you get a chance. They might decide to be kind."

"Will do. You don't need to pay for someone to pack up your personal items. I can handle that myself. The only difficulty will be making decisions about what items you want to keep but don't need immediately, and which ones you need right now."

"Any time you have a question, give me a call. I don't need anything from the kitchen—we bought most of the furnishings and kitchen items from thrift shops and didn't really have that much yet. Get some UPS boxes for the stuff I'll be keeping. I can rent a storage unit for it until I have a place of my own."

Judith shook her head. "No storage unit. Doug and I have decided to rent a three-bedroom house together, and it has plenty of storage in the garage and extra bedroom. Let me know whenever you need something, or make a trip over to get what you need right away."

Tiff looked up and grinned. "Cool."

"Don't get any ideas about our future," Judith said. "We like the idea of having more space and a yard for less than we're paying for our two apartments. Nothing else." She returned to the list but paused as their meals arrived.

"This looks wonderful," she exclaimed. Katie smiled. She had guessed Judith was a person who enjoyed good food.

"That's about all I put on the list," Tiff said as she toyed with her pasta. She gazed out the window. "It's almost dark and I don't see any sunset," she complained, taking a small bite.

Katie pointed at the horizon to their right. "I see a streak of color right there, and it appears to be spreading."

They stopped talking, barely eating as they watched the dark rose turn steadily pinker and slowly spread across the horizon, reflecting off the clouds higher in the sky, brightening and putting the mountains in sharp relief.

"Gorgeous," Judith exclaimed. "Thank you for bringing me here."

Twenty minutes later Judith had finished her ribeye steak, Katie boxed half of her seafood spaghetti to take home, and Tiff took most of her vegetable pasta with her.

"You'd better start eating better," Judith admonished Tiff on the way to the car. "You're eating for two now."

"I'll try," Tiff said. "It seems like my stomach has been upset for weeks, so it should start behaving better soon."

"Have you been to a doctor?" Katie asked, suddenly concerned.

"I have an appointment in a week. So much was going on, I didn't realize my almost constant nausea was because I was pregnant. It wasn't until after Phil died that I thought to do a pregnancy test."

"You don't sound too happy about it," Judith said with a frown.

Tiff shook her head. "I don't know how I feel. If Phil was still alive, we'd both be delighted. Even if Dad was alive, I could be happy for the joy a grandchild would give him. But now . . . I don't know. I'll have to start working soon, and that will be harder to do if I look fat."

"Well, get over it, girl," Judith admonished. "You are going to have this baby, and it is going to need you to love it and take care of it. Everything else will work out."

"I hope I'm allowed to do that," Tiff said, her voice barely a whisper.

The ride home was mostly silent. The dark obliterated the mountain view. Katie was thankful for the silence when she negotiated the hairpin turns that brought them back to Cactus City. She dropped

Judith off at the Switchback Motel and continued on to the rental.

Katie felt a chill on the back of her neck when they approached the rental. Something was wrong. She stopped the car before entering the driveway, trying to determine what it was.

"What's the matter, Katie?" Tiff asked, her voice querulous. "I'm tired, let's go in."

"The doorway light is out," Katie said.

"What? We probably forgot to turn it on."

"No, I know I turned it on before we left."

"So? It probably burned out."

Katie shook her head. "Maybe. But with everything that has been going on, I don't want to trust that it's a coincidence." She pulled out her cell phone, looked up her phone log, and hit the number for the police station.

"Oh, don't be silly. I want to go to bed," Tiff argued, getting out of the car and starting toward the unit.

"Cactus City police," a voice intoned in Katie's ear, startling her. At that same moment, Tiff opened the door to the rental and a blast sent her flying backward. Katie dropped the phone.

CHAPTER TWELVE

"May I help you?" the voice intoned, but Katie was already out of the car. She raced to Tiff and dropped to her knees. Relief swept through her when she heard a groan. Tiff was bleeding from several shallow cuts and gouges in her lovely face, but she was alive.

By the time Katie got back to the car and retrieved her cell phone, the police dispatcher had disconnected. When she dialed 911 the same voice responded.

"Need an ambulance," Katie managed to say.

"What is your address?"

Katie told her.

"Hold one minute," the dispatcher said. When she came back on the line, she assured Katie an ambulance was on its way. "Now, can you tell me what happened?" she asked.

"I don't know. I thought something was wrong when we got home, but my friend opened the door anyway, and something exploded."

"Then, you need the police too," the dispatcher said.

"Yes, of course. I'm sorry. I'm not thinking too clearly right now."

"Do you want me to stay on the line until they get there?"

While they were talking, Katie had gone back to Tiff. "No, I want to see what I can do to help Tiff," she said.

"Don't move her or anything until the EMTs can check her out," the dispatcher warned.

Promising she wouldn't, Katie disconnected and knelt back at Tiff's side, taking her hand. "Help is on the way," she said. "Hang in there."

Tiff didn't answer. She hadn't opened her eyes, but had stopped groaning and her breathing seemed to be steady. Katie stayed by her side until the ambulance arrived and the same EMTs who had come to the motel when Phil was murdered moved her out of their way. They checked Tiff over for a few minutes, during which time Chief Browning arrived.

"Don't you ever sleep?" Katie asked.

"Evidently not while you're in town," he replied.

The EMTs brought a gurney out and loaded Tiff onto it. "It doesn't look as if she has any serious injuries except most likely a concussion since she hasn't regained consciousness. We need to take her in for a more complete check."

"She's pregnant," Katie said.

"Thank you. We'll let the doctor know," the EMT said, making a note on his chart.

Chief Browning stepped back. "When did that happen?" he asked.

Katie had to choke back what threatened to be a fit of hysterical laughter. "She recently found out, using one of those pregnancy tests you get at the pharmacy. She has an appointment to see a doctor next week."

"So, maybe the baby's father helped her knock off her husband."

Anger smothered any possible laughter. Even with no evidence it was true, she was quite convinced she was right when she stated, "Phil is the baby's father. If you need to be convinced, a DNA test will prove it. In the meantime, I'll thank you not to smear a grieving widow's name. You might regret it."

The chief leaned back on his heels and looked down at Katie, a slight smile on his face. "Is that a threat, young lady?"

"Try me," she spat back.

A patrol car arrived and Chief Browning instructed the officers to inspect the house for any further risk.

"You'll need to give me the name of the owners of your rental."

Katie's heart sank. What were the owners going to do about a tenant who got their house blown up? But she had no choice. She pulled out her cell phone and located the information for the chief.

"You won't be able to stay here until that door is repaired," he said.

"I can stay with my grandmother." The thought of spending any time in that tiny house with that wee bathroom made her feel claustrophobic. "Or maybe a motel."

Thrift won. She wasn't short of money yet, but until she got a job, it would be wise to be more careful of her spending than she had ever been before.

When she arrived at Nana's house, the lights were still on. She knocked out of courtesy, but when there was no answer she let herself in with her key. She found her grandmother asleep in the recliner, the television broadcasting the news of the day. She was still in her robe from the morning.

She gently shook Nana's shoulder. "Nana? Can you wake up a minute?"

Her eyes fluttered open. "What are you doing here at this hour?"

"There was an accident at my rental. May I stay here with you tonight?"

"Of course. I'm comfortable where I am. Why don't you use the bed?"

Katie didn't want to argue with her about it now, so she retreated to the bedroom and collapsed.

Nana was still asleep when Katie got up after a restless night. Using the tiny bathroom was more of a challenge than Katie wanted to face, besides which she didn't have a change of clothes or any of her personal things.

Taking a chance that she would be able to get in, she drove back to the rental. There was tape across the doorway, but it hadn't been boarded up yet. She was about to try to maneuver her way through the tape when the young police officer appeared from around the side of the building.

Startled, she asked, "Have you been here all night?"

He gave her a rueful grin. "Unfortunately, yes. The fire department has not yet cleared the building and the chief doesn't want any possible evidence disturbed."

"Everything I own is in there," Katie objected. "I need some things right now."

The officer shook his head. "I'm sorry, I can't let you go in. It may only be a few hours before everything is cleared up, though. After that you will have access."

This young officer was far too nice for Katie to try to bully. She climbed back into her car and headed to the small general store on Main Street to get the things she needed. Returning to Nana's house, she managed to get ready for the day. Nana was still asleep.

Concerned about Tiff, after a quick breakfast of a fried egg on toast, Katie drove to the clinic, hoping Tiff hadn't been hurt badly enough to be sent to the hospital in Prescott or Phoenix. She was in luck. Tiff was not only at the clinic, she was awake and appeared to be alert.

"How are you feeling?" Katie asked, afraid to ask the hard question.

"Sore," Tiff answered with a rueful grin. "But lucky. The baby is fine. The doctor said it would take a harder blow than I suffered to dislodge a healthy baby from the womb. So, I guess I also learned that the baby is healthy."

"Did you have a concussion? It looked like you did."

"Well, yeah. The nurse told me you get a concussion, with, like, resulting damage, every time you hit your head. The only question is, how much damage? Even though it knocked me out, I don't appear to have any serious effects from the fall." She frowned. "Except the cuts on my face. I hope they don't scar. That wouldn't be good for getting modeling jobs."

"Well, the main news is good," Katie said, maintaining a steady look with effort. Granted, Tiff's concern about her looks wasn't vanity but rather the need to look good for her modeling work, but it did seem to Katie that the fact Tiff wasn't hurt worse and her baby was all right should be the only things on her mind right now. "The unit had very little damage, mostly around the door, so the explosive might have been as much to scare us as anything."

"Can we get back in?" Tiff asked.

"I don't know how soon we can do that. That young officer who keeps showing up wouldn't let me in this morning, but he said it was only until the fire department and the police had finished their investigation. I had to buy what I needed for today."

"I sure wish this useless police chief would let us leave town. He has no evidence against either of us—especially you. We could use Dad's house until all this is settled."

"Maybe you could," Katie said. "If Lila would let

you. But, I have to stay here for my grandmother." She wondered how many times she'd have to repeat that before Tiff remembered. "I've put applications in on three apartments in town. They aren't great, but I need a place to stay while I'm looking for work."

"Um, have you ever looked for an apartment before?" Tiff asked.

"Yes, my place in Seattle. I got it right out of law school."

"But you already had a good job before you got it."

"Yes. Are you saying I won't get an apartment before I have a job?"

"I think that is possible. Even though you have a good education and a good work history, that won't make finding a job in a small place like this any easier. In fact, it might make it harder. You could get lucky, but most landlords I've come across want at least six months of current employment history before renting to someone."

Katie felt her stomach clench. Had she put the cart before the horse, as Nana said? She didn't have much time left to find a job before her two-month lease was up. If she could even get back into the rental.

"Sounds like it's back to the drawing board," Katie said. She thought for a minute. "Let's hope one of the temporary agencies comes up with something. I should at least make enough to defray the cost of a motel room while I'm looking for a steady job, so I won't use up all of my reserves."

"Well, they aren't going to let me out of here until

they're convinced the concussion hasn't caused any serious brain damage," Tiff said. "Maybe by that time we can get back in."

While Katie hoped it was possible, she doubted the landlord would be open to it. What would any landlord think about tenants who got their property blown up?

"At least we should be able to get our possessions," Katie said.

―――――――――

Worried that Nana hadn't dressed yesterday, Katie went from the clinic back to her house to check on her.

She opened the door, ready to call out. She stopped short, heart thumping. Nana was in the same place she had been when Katie left this morning—the same recliner she had been in last night. How long had it been since she had moved?

Approaching the recliner, she got a clue. The smell of urine was overpowering, indicating her grandmother had not budged from her position in over twenty-four hours.

"Nana?" she cried, jiggling her shoulder. "It's time to get up."

Nana didn't respond. Panic gripped her; Katie shook harder. "Nana? Wake up!" Her voice was becoming shrill. Nana still didn't move.

Katie grabbed the landline phone and dialed 911.

"What is the nature of your emergency?" the dispatcher asked.

"I arrived at my grandmother's house to find her unresponsive. She hasn't moved from her chair since sometime yesterday."

After giving the woman the address, she collapsed on the floor beside the recliner and gripped her grandmother's hand, tears streaking down her cheeks. "I came here for you, Nana," she whispered. "Don't you go and die on me now."

CHAPTER THIRTEEN

Katie felt a sudden void, like a drop in the air pressure, when the sirens stopped. It took a moment to register that the ambulance had arrived. After checking Nana over, the EMTs, who by now must consider Katie a steady customer, efficiently whisked her grandmother onto a gurney and into the ambulance. Katie locked the door and followed them to the clinic, where a physicians' assistant checked Nana again and hooked her up to an IV.

"She's seriously dehydrated," the PA said. "We can do a CT scan and blood tests, but my guess is that she'll awaken as soon as we get enough fluids in her."

"Thank you," Katie said, her voice catching with relief. "She had an episode of falling a few days ago, so she has had a CT scan and blood tests. We'll be seeing Dr. Pelson as soon as he has the results."

"In that case, we'll keep an eye on her for now and see how she comes around with the IV before doing anything else."

Since Nana was still asleep, Katie went down the hall where she found Tiff reclining on the raised head of her bed, long blonde hair hanging over her shoulders in soft waves. The shadows under her saucer-like blue eyes were less pronounced, but she had three lines of feathery stitches across her cheeks.

"You look good," Katie said.

"Yeah, I'll be fine." Tiff smiled an angelic smile Katie had never seen on her face before. "It is so wonderful I got pregnant before I lost Phil and his father. This scare taught me I have someone I want to live for."

"Or maybe you're happy you will have someone you might be able to control, who will inherit from both of them after you are convicted of murder," a voice growled from behind Katie.

Katie whirled around. Chief Browning, an unlit stub of a cigar sticking out of his shirt pocket, stood back on his heels, thumbs stuck in his low-hanging belt.

"Really, Chief Browning? Someone tried to kill Tiff—or me —or both of us," she said. "You might let up a little bit now."

The chief snorted. "That explosive wasn't much more than a firecracker and hardly damaged anything except the door. Maybe you did it yourself to throw us off. Maybe someone was trying to scare you. Whatever, it obviously wasn't meant to kill."

Katie stared at him. "Tiff suffered a concussion from that 'firecracker.' She has scars on her face that will affect her life as a model. And," her voice dropped nearly to a whisper, "she could have lost the baby."

"So, what's your theory?" he asked, his lips turned up in a derisive sneer.

Katie paced the three steps she could manage in the small room. "I think someone wants Tiff to lose the baby."

The sneer turned into a bark of laughter. "How would anyone, except maybe you, know that Mrs. Wells would go to the door first?"

Pacing some more, Katie tried to think it through. "If I had gone to the door first, they probably would have found a way to make it look as though Tiff did it, the same way they set her up for the murder charge. The only hope the real murderer has is to get rid of the baby and still have Tiff convicted, all the while managing to stay out of the limelight."

"Of all the half-assed stories I ever heard, that one takes the cake," Chief Browning said. "I suppose you think you know who did it?"

"What about Jeffrey?" Tiff asked.

"Jeffrey has an alibi for both murders."

Tiff's brows knit. "He could have hired someone. And does he have an alibi for the 'firecracker'?"

"Now you are really stretching. I believe that when we check, we'll find out Jeffrey was in Phoenix yesterday and the day before."

Katie shook her head. It was probably true that Jeffrey's alibis were solid. Besides, under the provisions of Mr. Wells' amendment to his trust, Jeffrey wouldn't gain anything by preventing Tiffany from getting her share. For some reason, she felt good about the possibility of eliminating him as a suspect. "What about Lila?" she asked.

"Who?"

Katie stared at him. "Lila. Mr. Wells' new wife. Surely you know about her."

"Oh, the wife," he said. "Why would she want to hurt Tiffany Wells or her baby?"

"Because Mr. Wells did not leave his wife everything. Even though she signed a prenuptial agreement, she might think she could get her hands on a lot more if Tiff and the baby were out of the way." She frowned. That didn't make sense either. She would probably still only get her million, no matter what happened with Tiffany.

Chief Browning glared at her. "The reason I stopped by," he finally said, "is because someone tried to gain access to the crime scene this morning."

"That would be me," Katie said. "I wanted to remove personal belongings, which had nothing to do with the crime, but your officer wouldn't let me enter."

"Well, the fire department and the police are finished with the scene now, so you can get your stuff. In fact, your landlord wants you to get out of there as soon as possible, before any more damage is done to his place."

"I don't suppose he offered to refund the rest of my rent money?"

"Ha! After what happened to his property? You'll be lucky if he doesn't sue you. You can ask him about it when you arrange to get your things."

"He has insurance to cover the damage, and I didn't do anything to be sued for. I'll be looking into that refund."

"Good luck with that, Ms. Fancy-Pants-Lawyer." He strode out of the room.

"Do you know when you can leave the clinic?" Katie asked Tiff.

"The doctor said possibly tomorrow, if the dizziness from the concussion is gone. It is getting better. But I don't know where to go."

"I don't know if the police can make you stay in Cactus City, since they haven't charged you with anything, but I have to be with my grandmother. She has to stay here to see her doctor and get herself back to normal." Katie felt a tremor of fear. What if there was no back to normal for Nana? "I have to find another place to live," she added. "If you don't want to go to Phoenix, do you want to get a place together? Maybe we can find another short-term rental, since you don't know what you'll be doing when all this is over."

"That might be too dangerous for you. If whoever is doing this tries again . . ."

Katie felt her last bit of resistance to playing detective melt away. If either she or Tiff was going to be able to start any kind of new life, they had to get rid of this threat. They would certainly not get any help from Chief Browning.

"Have you heard from Mr. Leighton about that letter Phil's father sent him?" she asked.

"Yes," Tiff said. "He called to tell me he had talked with Mr. Morley, who knew nothing about it. Mr.

Morley is going to look for the amendment to the trust in Dad's home office. Why?"

Katie didn't want to say too much until she had a better idea what she was doing. "I'd like to find out what the story is behind this foundation he left the residue of his estate to," she said. "And I'd also like to know how much money we're talking about."

Tiff's expression hardened. "I still think Jeffrey is the cause of the problems we've been having. A million and a half isn't enough for him. He wants it all. Besides, how much more could there be?"

Katie shook her head. Tiff would not be convinced that Jeffrey had nothing to gain by getting rid of her. "I doubt that you have any idea how much Mr. Wells was worth," she said. "Maybe Mr. Morley could shed some light on that. Do you have his number?"

Tiff looked thoughtful for a moment, then brightened. "Oh, it's on my phone, in my purse, which I dropped in the explosion. Do you know if the police found it?"

"I'll ask. If they didn't, I'll go look for it after I check on Nana again."

Katie felt like a ping-pong ball as she headed back down the hall. Nana had not awakened. Katie was relieved to see that someone had cleaned her up, so she looked and smelled fresh.

Katie called the police station and learned the police had not found Tiff's purse, but they had not searched very far from the house since they had only been looking for clues the bomber might have left.

After planting a soft kiss on Nana's forehead, Katie

went to the nurse's station. "I have an errand I need to run," she said. "I'll be back as soon as I can."

"That's fine," a nurse said. "You can't do anything for her now, anyway."

———————

Katie discovered that the rental's doorway had been boarded over with plywood. She skirted around the side, but was disappointed to find the back door into the laundry room locked. Her key didn't work on that door, which blew her hope to retrieve their belongings before facing the landlord.

Going to the spot where Tiff had been propelled by the force of the blast, Katie began walking around in concentric circles, first on driveway stones and then on scrubby ground. A few minutes later she spotted Tiff's purse under a shrub of manzanita.

A chill slid down her back. She peered around, feeling exposed, but didn't see anything that could have caused it. Grabbing the purse, she hurried to her car and locked the door. She glanced toward the rental as she pulled out of the driveway but didn't see anything to cause her unease.

Once she was far enough away to feel safe, she pulled over and found the landlord's number on her phone, called, and arranged to get their belongings out later that afternoon. Afterward, she would start working to get her rent back.

_____

Tiff frowned when she pulled her cell phone out of her purse.

"What is it?" Katie asked.

"I'm not sure. Something doesn't seem right, but I can't figure out what it is."

"Do you think someone has been in your purse?" Katie asked, remembering the chill she had felt.

Tiff shook her head. "Everything is here, even the money in this zipped pocket. I must be feeling spooked, that's all."

Katie was reluctant to go to Chief Browning with such a nebulous worry. She was sure he wouldn't do anything about it. "You should take everything out and put it back the way it belongs," she said. "That's probably the only way you can know for sure if something's missing. In the meantime, I need to go check on my grandmother."

Trudging once more down the hall, she found Nana awake, but she barely responded to Katie's entry into the room.

A stab of anxiety pierced Katie. "Is she going to be all right?" she asked the nurse who was taking Nana's blood pressure.

"Doctor Pelson is here. I'll ask him to come and talk to you."

Katie sat for a few minutes at the side of the bed, gently stroking Nana's hand until the doctor arrived and motioned Katie out to the hallway.

"Your grandmother had a small stroke," Dr. Pelson

said. "From the CT scan we did yesterday, we can see she has had several mini-strokes, called TIAs, in the last year or so. That fall she had seems to have caused a brain bleed, resulting in swelling, which exacerbated this one."

"What do we do now?" Katie asked.

The doctor shook his head. "There isn't much we can do. If you can tell one is coming on and can get her in here quickly, we might be able to give her something to alleviate it. Usually though, by the time a patient arrives, it is too late to do anything except keep an eye on her to see if anything more serious is going to happen."

"Is she likely to have another one? Can she lead a normal life?"

"We'll have to see how well she recovers. It'll take time, and probably therapy to recover from any muscle and memory damage. With her history, we can't tell if and when she'll have another episode. Do you live with her?"

"No. Her house is too small for two people."

"As soon as we're sure your grandmother is stabilized, we'll send her to rehab. When they release her, she'll need someone to stay with her, at least for a while. If you can't arrange to do that, I suggest a nursing home, where she can continue rehab. We'll see about in-home healthcare when she gets a little stronger. Looking to the future, you need to consider the possibility that if she has a more serious stroke she might need twenty-four-hour care."

"Is that likely to happen?" Katie managed through a constricted throat.

"Unfortunately, with a history of small strokes, the chances are good that she will have a more damaging one at some point. We have no way of knowing when that might be, or even how damaging her current brain bleed is."

When Katie returned to her grandmother, Nana looked at her with unfocused eyes. "Want to go home," she whispered.

"As soon as possible, Nana," Katie said, hoping she could make it happen. "As soon as possible."

CHAPTER FOURTEEN

Tiff had finished straightening her purse and was just getting off the phone with Mr. Morley when Katie returned to her room. She handed Katie her car keys. "In case you need to get my things out of the rental. Nothing was taken," she added. "I don't know who would rummage around in my purse without taking anything."

"We never thought robbery was the motive," Katie said. "If anything interested them, they probably photographed it."

———————

When Katie left the clinic, she needed to think. She couldn't imagine being able to do that while cramped up in Nana's tiny house. Since the rental was out of bounds, she opted for the Top View Bar.

"Well, hello," Marta said. "I'm glad to see you again."

"Thank you. I needed a little peace and space to figure out some things. This seemed like the best place to do it."

"I'm so pleased you think of us in that regard." She led Katie to a secluded table well away from the room where the TV blared the current sports game. "What can I get to help you figure things out?"

Katie looked at her watch and was surprised to discover it was mid-afternoon already. While a double shot of bourbon on the rocks was tempting, it was a little early to start drinking, especially on an empty stomach. Besides, she had to meet the landlord later.

"It looks like I missed lunch," she said. "How about some sweet potato fries and a glass of iced tea?"

"You've got it," said Marta, turning back to the bar.

Katie rubbed her forehead with her fingertips, feeling a headache coming on. She had left her high-paying job in Seattle, in a way that pretty much assured she would never get another one like it, because of the stress it had caused. That stress paled compared to what she was facing now.

Marta brought her iced tea. "The fries will be out in a minute. We're not busy at this time of day, so if you need a listening ear, let me know."

"Thank you," Katie said with a smile. Hearing those words seemed to make her load a little lighter. She dug in her purse for her always present pad and pen. She had succeeded in her job because she knew how to prioritize, and that was exactly what she needed to do now.

First, of course, she needed to find a place to live. That might not be so easy when potential landlords learned about the explosion. And, if she found something, it had to be large enough for Tiff to live with her temporarily, and maybe accommodate Nana in the future. She took a sip of her iced tea.

She made a note to let Robert know what was going on with Nana, and the decisions they might have to make in a few days.

Next on the list was a job. She took a larger gulp of her iced tea and winced. Bourbon would have been a lot better. It was obvious to her now that she would be overqualified for most of the jobs available in this small city, and not have the specific qualifications needed for the rest of them. Prescott and Phoenix were both too far away as long as Nana might need her.

Of course, topping all of these things was figuring out who was responsible for Phil's and his father's deaths. If it wasn't Tiff and it wasn't Jeffrey, or Lila, who could it be? While she felt good about ruling Jeffrey out, she wasn't so sure about Lila. If the woman was wily enough to get Jim Wells to marry her, what else might she have up her sleeve? Also, Katie needed to learn more about the foundation that stood to receive "the residue," however much that was.

Marta returned with Katie's sweet potato fries and sat in the chair across from her. "Word travels fast in a small town," she said. "I know a lot about what has happened to you. I'm not sure why you became entangled in Tiffany Wells' problems, but I can see that you are a person who won't abandon her to the system. So, if there is any way I can help, you only need to ask."

"My most pressing need is to find a place to live," Katie said. "My grandmother's house is so tiny it could hardly suffice for one of us, and I think Tiff and I need to stay together until this is cleared up. I'm hoping the explosion at the vacation rental doesn't discourage landlords from renting to us."

Katie's cell phone rang. It was the owner of one of the apartments she had applied for. "I'm afraid we can't afford the risk," he said. "You have no source of income and we need a year's lease."

She was sure she was going to hear the same thing or something similar from the other two apartments.

Marta went to the front of the bar and came back with a real estate flyer. "Look through this and see if there is anything you would be interested in," she suggested.

And can afford, Katie thought.

When Marta went to wait on other customers, Katie leafed through the paper. It was hard not to look at the beautiful houses with mountain views but, even in Cactus, those were outside her current, largely nonexistent, budget. She circled four with prices she might be able to manage.

Marta came back with a refill of iced tea. She looked at the listings Katie had circled, then pointed to a Realtor further down the page. "It's not too late to call real estate agents, you know. Especially this one, who's right here in town and is open on Sunday."

"What if I need some time to think about it?"

"You can think while you're looking."

Katie made the call when Marta went off to serve another customer. The receptionist put her through to the Realtor, Carolyn Taylor, who said she would see Katie in her office at four-thirty that afternoon to get basic information and possibly arrange to show Katie something tomorrow.

It was time to meet the landlord. When he arrived at the rental, he silently produced a key to the laundry room door. Katie had to make several trips around the side to move everything into her car and Tiff's.

When she had finished, she said, "I was here less than a week. I paid for two month's rent. When can I expect a refund for the rest of the rent?"

"Refund? It will take more than the amount you paid to repair the damage to my property."

"Damage I didn't cause, and which you must have insurance to cover," Katie retorted. "If you don't want to refund my rent, I'll be happy to return and finish my lease after you repair the damage."

"What if whoever has it in for you causes more damage? No. I don't want to take that chance."

"Nevertheless, we have a contract for two month's rent. Either I have use of the unit or I get my rent back."

"You can talk to my attorney," the landlord retorted.

After locking the laundry room door, he got into his car and sped away.

———————

Walking into Nana's house, Katie could smell the urine that had soaked into the recliner cushions. She should have cleaned it up earlier. She removed the cushions, put them outside the door, wondering if airing them out would take care of the odor. She sprayed the house with air freshener she found under the kitchen sink, stripped the bed, and gathered up dirty clothing and towels to start the first load of laundry. She wondered how long it had been since Nana had done laundry. There would be at least three loads, even without worrying about separating colored clothing from whites the way her mother had taught her to do.

She could barely get the bed made up with fresh sheets before collapsing into it and immediately falling into a deep sleep.

Katie awoke to pounding on the door. Squinting through blurry eyes, she discovered it was almost four o'clock. She had slept for about half an hour. Whoever it was had awakened her from an obviously needed nap but had also prevented her from missing her appointment with the Realtor. She dragged herself out of bed and stumbled to the door. With no peephole, she had no choice but to open it.

"What are you trying to do to me?"

"Jeffrey! What are you doing here? How did you find me?"

"Don't pretend innocence. Someone tried to kill me, and it had to be Tiffany. Where is she?" He looked over her shoulder as if expecting to see Tiff lurking in the background.

Katie shook her head to clear it. Had she heard correctly? "What? When? Tiffany has been in the clinic since yesterday as a result of a bomb planted at my rental unit."

Jeffrey stared at her for a moment. He seemed to be trying to absorb the news. "Well, if she didn't do it herself, she must have hired someone."

"That sounds suspiciously like what we were saying about you. But, you both get a million and a half. Isn't that enough?"

"I think that demented girl's brain tells her she can still get my share too." He turned and strode back toward the street.

"Wait! Jeffrey, we need to talk about this!" she cried. "Who told you I was at my grandmother's?"

Without acknowledging the question, he continued walking to a new Chevy Caprice with rental plates on it and drove away.

Katie stared after the car. He appeared to know nothing about the bomb at her rental. Was someone else threatening Tiff, and Jeffrey too? Of course, he could be faking a threat in order to muddy the waters.

CHAPTER FIFTEEN

A glance at her watch made Katie forget about Jeffrey. Her appointment with Carolyn Taylor was in less than half an hour. She wedged herself into the cramped bathroom for a quick shower, then pulled on a clean pair of jeans and a sweater.

She arrived at Carolyn's office with a minute to spare. The receptionist led her from the small but tidy outer office to an equally small but tidy inner office where a woman with a wiry build; short, bleached, feathery hair; and sharp-blue eyes stood to greet her.

"Carolyn Taylor," she said. After taking Katie's financial information and house requirements, she sat back and thought for a moment. "You can obviously pay a large percentage of the price up front to buy an inexpensive house, but the mortgage holder will want assurance that you'll be able to continue payments on the remainder."

"Well, my work history won't improve much for

a while because I'll be doing temporary work until I can find a permanent position. I do have a friend who may be living with me for a short time. She is also not working, but she has probably inherited a sizeable estate."

Carolyn's eyebrows shot up. "Probably?"

Katie sighed. She didn't know how much of Tiff's personal information she should divulge. But Tiff also needed a place to stay. After she had explained the situation, Carolyn was silent, tapping her pencil on her desk. "It won't hurt to start looking while she gets her finances figured out. Are you free tomorrow morning, say ten o'clock?"

"Tomorrow morning at ten should be fine."

From Carolyn's office, Katie went to the clinic where she found Tiff ready to be released as soon as they got the final paperwork from the doctor. Katie continued to her grandmother's room.

Nana smiled when Katie entered. Her eyes hadn't recovered their customary sharpness, but they weren't as unfocused as they had been yesterday.

"Going home?" she asked.

"As soon as possible, Nana," Katie said, "but the doctor thinks you need some time to work out the kinks from that little stroke you had."

"I had a stroke?" Her brow furrowed.

"Didn't Dr. Pelson talk to you?" Katie asked, looking up as a nurse entered the room. The nurse nodded.

"I don't remember. So, I have to stay here?"

"Yes, for right now." To distract her from objecting,

Katie went on quickly, "Is it all right if I stay in your house for a little while?"

"Of course, dear. Will that friend of yours be staying too?"

"I don't think so. Your house is a little small for two people. We'll see if she can manage something else."

Nana smiled as her eyes closed. "Whatever you think is best, dear," she managed before drifting off to sleep.

On her way back to Tiff's room, Katie stopped at the visitor's lounge for her overdue call to Robert.

"Nana had a mini-stroke," she said. "The doctor wants her to go to a nursing home for rehab when she leaves the clinic. She signed an agreement giving me her health power of attorney, but her attorney thinks Nana made it clear you are the one to make other decisions for her."

"I'll be there as soon as I can get a flight. See if you can get us in to see Nana's attorney on Wednesday."

"Oh, thank you, Robert. I could sure use my big brother's support right now. I'll arrange for a motel room and I'll text you when it's done."

As soon as she disconnected, she called Mrs. Andrews' office, hoping to leave a message. She was surprised when the attorney answered the phone.

"I'm not in my office. I have calls forwarded to me," she said. "What can I do for you?"

Katie explained that Robert was coming and asked if it would be possible to see her Wednesday and clarify things.

"If you can get in at eight in the morning, I'll fit you in before my first appointment."

Katie thanked her and continued to Tiff's room. Tiff waved a sheaf of papers at her. "Let's get out of here. But, where are we going?"

"Let's get your car and go to the Switchback. I need to get a room for my brother, and you can get one too." She held her breath, waiting to see if Tiff would object to the expense.

"Sounds good," Tiff said, heading for the door, where an orderly intercepted her with a wheelchair and wheeled her the rest of the way out.

Katie released her breath with relief.

While Katie drove to the vacation rental so Tiff could get her car, she told Tiff about Jeffrey's visit.

"What happened? And what made him think I did it?" Tiff asked.

"He didn't explain, he just assumed it was you. But, I don't think I'm mistaken that he was shocked to hear about the bombing. I hope we can get him to listen so we can all try to figure out what is really going on."

Tiff sniffed; a decidedly uncool sound. "I'm not interested in anything he has to say. I still think he killed Phil and Dad and tried to blame it on me so he could get all Dad's money."

"Well, I'm not so sure anymore. We need to find out what the story is with this foundation Mr. Wells suddenly became interested in."

When they got to the Switchback Motel, Katie reserved a room for Robert and put in a call to the police station while Tiff was arranging for her room.

"Do you know if someone there told Jeffrey Crane that I was staying at my grandmother's house?" she asked the officer who answered the phone.

"Yes. I overheard Chief Browning mention where you were staying to Mr. Crane when he was here to report the sabotage on his car."

Katie wanted to explode, but this was not the person she wanted to explode at. "Please, let Chief Browning know that I don't appreciate his giving out my private information," she managed in a tight voice.

"Well, I could use a good, stiff drink about now," Katie said after helping Tiff take her belongings to her room. "I think I'll go to the Top View to have it."

"Can I go with you?" Tiff asked.

"If you want to. You don't have to drink, but it may not be comfortable for you."

Tiff frowned. "I can't drink?"

"Tiffany Wells, you are pregnant. Have you not heard that drinking is bad for your baby?"

"Well, I guess. But nobody I know ever stopped drinking and I never saw anything wrong with their babies."

"So, you're willing to take the chance?"

The uncertainty was still on Tiff's face when she shrugged. "No, I guess not. I don't want to do anything that will harm Phil's baby. But I'd like to join you. Do they have food?"

"Bar food, but we'll get a handle on your diet another day," Katie said with a laugh. "We can't stay long. I have an appointment with a Realtor to look at houses at ten tomorrow morning. I know you don't usually get out that early, but if you think you might want to stay in Cactus for a while, you could go with me."

Tiff brightened. "We might find a place where we can live together."

Katie wasn't sure that was what she wanted, even though it might be necessary in order to get a place.

———————

"This is kind of a dump," Tiff said when they entered the bar.

"It's rustic," Katie snapped. "It feels comfortable to me."

Marta walked up with Katie's drink as soon as they sat at their table.

"What can I get you?" she asked Tiff.

Tiff eyed Katie's bourbon and sighed. "Tonic water with a twist. Do you have anything decent to eat?"

Marta's voice was cold when she replied. "All of our food is decent." She handed Tiff a menu.

Tiff frowned as she read the menu. "Nothing looks good to me," she said, shoving it back at Marta when she returned with her tonic water. "It's all greasy bar food."

"This is a bar," Marta said. Her voice was now icy. "If you want restaurant food, go to a restaurant." She stomped away.

"She doesn't have to be so snooty," Tiff complained, sipping her drink and making a face.

Suddenly Katie wasn't sure she wanted to buy a house with this woman.

———————

Katie picked Tiff up at the motel the next morning and drove to Carolyn's office. "I hope you aren't expecting too much," Carolyn said as she escorted Tiff and Katie to her gray BMW. "None of the houses you picked out are in prime condition."

The first stop was a house with a woodsy exterior and pleasant feel. Carolyn didn't even open her car door. Instead she pointed at the dense brush around the house and said, "Fire is the main threat to property in this dry, wooded area. It appears no one has taken any efforts to safeguard this house from fire in a lot of years."

The second yard was clear of brush, but the advertising photo had not revealed the dilapidated mobile home behind the roomy deck.

They did enter the third house. It was nearer to the city and had a neighborhood feel to it; plus, it seemed to be in good repair. The interior was another matter. The strong odor indicated it had been home to untrained pets.

"I think you can see that you'll have to go higher in price," Carolyn said. "I have two more properties to show you that have open houses today."

The houses were in modest but neat neighborhoods, in the flat area south of town. They were both two-bedroom homes. The less expensive one had one bath, the other had two.

Katie shook her head. "The price on both of these is more than I'm comfortable with."

"I'd like to take you back to my office and go over some financials with you."

Katie glanced at her watch. "Not today. My brother is coming from Seattle and should be at my grandmother's house soon."

"No problem. Why don't we meet there to talk? I understand your grandmother might be going into a nursing home. If her house is too small for you, you might be looking at putting it on the market. I can help you with that."

"My grandmother's house will not be going on the market anytime soon," Katie said, her voice sharper than she intended. "And, I don't have time to talk now. I'll be in touch if we decide to keep looking for a house."

"Well, that was a waste of time," Tiff said when they had left Carolyn's office and were headed to Katie's car.

Katie jerked to a stop and peered around, her chest tightening.

"What?" Tiff asked.

Katie pointed at the car. Someone had flattened the left rear tire. Closing her eyes and taking a deep breath, she tried to calm herself. The tire was flat. That didn't mean someone had done it. Anyway, no one was there now. Pulling out her cell phone, Katie called AAA.

The mechanic who arrived put on the spare and took the flat tire. "I'll see if this can be repaired, but we won't be able to get to it today," he said. "You can drive with the spare until we do."

———————

Robert was waiting at the house when they arrived. Katie jumped out of the car and ran to him, doing her best to envelop him in a hug, even though he was several inches taller and broader than she was.

"I am so glad you came," she said. "Everything that could go wrong has since I got here. If I hadn't done such a thorough job of burning my bridges in Seattle, I might be tempted to throw in the towel and go back to my old life."

"I don't know if there was a better way to handle your problems there," Robert said, "but now we have to figure out how to make your new situation work for you."

"Let's get you settled in at the Switchback Motel, grab a late lunch, and spend the rest of the afternoon with Nana at the clinic," Katie said. "After that, we'll go to the Top View Bar where we can relax and talk."

Tiff and Katie rode with Robert in his rental car. After checking him in at the motel, they dropped his bag off in his room.

"We are going to the ZigZag Café for lunch," Katie told Tiff. "Do you want to join us?"

"No. I think the little one wants a rest," Tiff said.

"Besides, you two have lots to talk about. Give me a call when you leave your grandmother."

"Sounds good to me," Robert said. "I'm starving, and I'm also anxious to see Nana."

They settled at their table in the café and both ordered the Western Salad special of the day.

"I'm glad we have a chance to talk," Robert said. "I'm a little surprised Nana is not in a hospital. Can she get the best care at the clinic?"

"I think so," Katie said, trying to keep a lid on her annoyance. Robert was questioning her judgment already? "I did some research and discovered Dr. Pelson made news when he moved to this small city to set up a facility where people could get most of their medical needs met in a convenient location. It is more than urgent care, but not quite a hospital. He doesn't hesitate to send patients to Yavapai Regional Medical Center if he can't handle their care here."

"Don't you think we should get a second opinion?"

"We could do that. Would you trust another doctor in Cactus City or do we have to take her to YRMC in Prescott Valley?"

"Can she be moved?"

"I don't know. She is getting stronger, so she might be able to handle a car ride."

"I think we should see another doctor in Cactus City before tackling that."

"Fine," Katie said. "We'll look into that tomorrow."

They spent a long time over lunch, talking about their mother and Pete's adoption plans. Katie hadn't had much time to get to know the boys, but Robert was enthusiastic about them.

"For the amount of time they spent on the streets, they are amazing. Benjamin adores Mom and Mom is ecstatic that he shares her artistic talent. Eric still seems to feel he has to be responsible for Benjamin, but Pete is gradually getting him to relax and be the little boy he's supposed to be."

When they finished their lunch, they headed for the clinic. "It's certainly a modern-looking building," Robert said as they approached it. "Does it have state-of-the-art equipment?"

"They can do CAT scans and MRIs, which are the most useful for checking Nana's condition."

Katie had always been so stressed when coming to the clinic that she had never given it a good look before. It was, indeed, modern and immaculate, inside and out. Dr. Pelson had achieved something quite uncommon for this type of location.

They walked down the squeaky-clean hallway to Nana's room, where Nana seemed to be resting easily, her eyes closed and her face at peace. Someone had taken the time to wash her hair, and it spread about her head like a halo. Katie pressed a hand to her arm.

"Nana? Can you wake up? Robert is here to see you."

Her eyes opened and a smile spread across her face. Alarmed, Katie looked at Robert, her heart thumping. It was immediately apparent that the smile was a little lopsided.

"Robert. When?" Nana managed in a whispery voice, her hand shaking as she reached out for him.

"I got here a few minutes ago," Robert said. "I can't stay long, but I want to see you getting better before I leave."

Nana nodded and drifted back to sleep with the smile still on her face.

Robert pulled Katie out of the room, where they found the nurse.

"Has she had another mini-stroke?" Katie asked.

"We think so. She was so much better earlier today."

"Could this have been avoided if she was in a hospital?" Robert demanded.

The nurse shook her head. "No. There is nothing they can do at a hospital that we can't do here."

"Will she hear us if we stay and talk with her?" Katie asked.

The nurse shook her head. "Most likely she could if it was only the stroke, but the doctor gave her a mild sedative to keep her comfortable, so she probably won't hear you now."

They stayed for a while, anyway. Nana had acknowledged Robert, so she was still aware. Robert talked to her about his fiancé, Olivia, and their plans for the future. The smile stayed on Nana's lips until she started breathing deeply and they decided she could no longer hear them.

Katie felt tears threatening when they returned to the car. "She fell and hit her head the first day I was here. I think she was fine before that and she seemed to be recovering from the fall nicely. I don't know if the fall had anything to do with these apparent strokes, but I feel like it has all happened because I came."

"Whoa," Robert said. "Did she even know you were here before she fell?"

"No."

"Well, I think that you were fortunate to get here before she had a stroke, and the fall could have hastened the stroke, so it's good you were here."

Katie smiled through the tears. "Thanks, big brother. I needed that."

When they arrived at the Top View Bar, Katie phoned Tiff, but Tiff said she wasn't feeling well and would stay at the motel. Marta showed them to the corner table, her hair flowing around her face in soft waves and her brown eyes shining. A moment later she placed a double bourbon on the rocks and a glass of water in front of Katie and turned to Robert.

"Scotch and water," he said, frowning at Katie's glass when Marta went to fetch his. "That looks like a double. And she remembers what you want. How many of those do you drink?"

"I appreciate my big brother being here but I hope he isn't going to start trying to manage my life."

"No, but you did tell me you were having some problems with addictive stuff in Seattle."

Her voice raised a notch. "Right. And I've totally rearranged my life to get away from it. I don't think I'm going to jeopardize that by becoming an alcoholic, but mostly I have more pressing things to worry about right now."

Robert raised his hands in surrender. "Sorry. I don't know if running away from your problems was the right thing to do, but it's your life. Maybe it was meant to be, so you would be here for Nana. At any rate, I'm sure you can take care of yourself."

"Thank you." She took a deep breath. It didn't sound like he thought she made good decisions, but she didn't want to get into an argument about it.

Marta brought Robert's drink. "How did house hunting go today?" she asked.

"Not well. The three houses I selected were not possible. The Realtor showed us two more. One might work, but it was ten thousand dollars more than what I want to spend."

"Do you need some financial help?" Robert asked.

"Aren't you planning a wedding pretty soon?" Katie countered.

"Well, yes, but if you need money ..."

"I don't know what I need yet, Robert, but thank you for the offer. Marta, I feel like spending the evening here. Do you have anything we could eat for dinner in an hour or so?"

"We don't do a full menu, but our burgers and fries are pretty good."

"That'll do," Robert said. "Not on my normal diet, but that makes me enjoy them more when I do have them."

"Let me know when you want me to put the order

in. May I barge in for a minute?" she asked, shifting from foot to foot as if she couldn't contain her excitement.

"Please, join us," Katie said.

"I want to tell you this right now because I think it'll help you. When I told my date last night about your situation, he told me he came here to check on a house his friend recently bought. His friend wants to flip it, but it needs some work. Fred, my date, says his friend doesn't have the funds to work on it right now, so she would like to rent it out for a while. It has two bedrooms and two baths. Is that perfect, or what? If you want to look at it, his friend is ready to rent it to you at a real good rate so she doesn't have to worry about it being vacant."

"Marta," Katie asked, afraid to let her hopes rise, "does this friend know the last place I rented was bombed?"

"They know all about it. While his friend hopes that doesn't happen to her house, she says she has insurance in case it does. Knowing your situation, she thinks you'll agree to go month to month on rent so that when she's ready to start working on it you can find something else." Her smile could have lit up Carnegie Hall. "I know you'll need time to think about it, and you also need time with your brother right now, but I wanted to let you know."

Katie stared at Robert when Marta bounced away. "What are the chances we could solve one of my problems so easily?"

"Kate, you don't know anything about these people."

Katie frowned. "For some reason, I think I can trust Marta."

"But you don't know her friend, or the owner. Use your lawyer instincts. Look at all the possible angles for why the owner would make such an offer."

Katie knew Robert was right. Her pressing need to find housing made her vulnerable. But Marta seemed to believe her date and his friend were trustworthy, and Katie trusted Marta. But did Katie know Marta well enough to trust her judgment in men?

CHAPTER SIXTEEN

Katie beckoned Marta back to their table.

"Marta, could we meet your boyfriend and look at the house tomorrow? I'll want Robert's advice about what to do."

Robert's brown eyes widened, almost making Katie laugh out loud. She had never asked Robert for advice about anything in her life. Until she had to start making decisions about Nana, of course.

Marta blinked, but her smile didn't lose any wattage. "Of course. I should have realized you couldn't jump in without more information. You don't know Fred. And, he's not really my boyfriend. I only met him two days ago. But, I think he is something special." She pulled out a business card and wrote a number on the back. "Here is my card, and Fred's number is on the back."

"You do catering?" Katie exclaimed, looking at the front of the card.

"Nothing fancy, but if you're putting on a casual party and need some help, I'm your gal. I couldn't do much more than that and help run this place, too, but it's a little extra cash."

After another round of drinks and finishing their burgers, Robert drove Katie back to Nana's house. "I'm going in first," he said. "I don't like all these things that are happening to you."

Katie glared at him. "So, they should happen to you, instead?" she snapped.

Robert grinned at her and got out of the car. "Still the same old Kate," he said.

They ended up going into the house together and finding everything as she had left it. Robert looked around and shook his head. "This place seems to get tinier every time I visit. I know you are a lot smaller than I am, but I can see why you need a different place to live, even if Nana ..."

"Don't say it," Katie whispered. Robert wrapped her in a bear hug, then left to go to the motel.

———

The next morning Katie rose early. She went out for a quick run and was pleased to discover she could do a gentle lope without becoming short of breath. When she returned to the house, she eyed the miniscule bathroom and had to restrain herself from calling Tiff to see if she could borrow the nice big bathroom in her motel room.

After she had managed to shower and eat a bowl of oatmeal, she went to the motel. Robert wasn't there. A quick call to his cell phone let her know he was already at the hospital.

She wanted to go there, too, but decided to check on Tiff first. As soon as Katie entered Tiff's room, Tiff pulled out her cell phone. She told Katie that she was anxious to find out if Mr. Leighton had heard anything more. She had waited until Katie arrived so she could be in on the call. When Mr. Leighton answered the phone, Tiff pushed the speaker button so Katie could hear.

"Mr. Morley hasn't sent me any more information about Mr. Wells' estate. So far, no formal charges have been brought against you, Tiffany, so I believe you'll have full access to your share once the addendum to the trust is found. However, if we push for it and the authorities don't agree, they might decide to file formal charges so you can't touch it. In which case, you might end up in jail."

"So, I have to wait?" Tiff's voice came out in a whine. "Neither one of us has enough money to support ourselves for long. We're looking for jobs, but we have no place to live."

"You have no funds in your own name?"

Tiff shook her head, twirling a strand of hair around her finger. "Not much. Phil took care of all the big stuff, and I only kept enough for my personal needs. The money in our joint account won't last very long."

"All right, I'll contact Mr. Morley to try and expedite

things. In the meantime, you need to go ahead and find whatever work you can. It will look good should the charges go any further."

"Time for me to go see how Nana is doing," Katie said when they disconnected.

"May I go with you?" Tiff asked. "I don't have anything else to do and I don't feel like being alone."

Katie reluctantly agreed. Tiff stayed in the waiting room to read a magazine while Katie went to Nana's room. When she arrived, Robert did not have the relieved and happy look Katie had been hoping for. Nana was sleeping, so Katie planted a kiss on her forehead before she and Robert retreated to the waiting room where they found a pot of coffee.

"The doctor was here earlier and told me the swelling from Nana's brain bleed was worse," Robert said. "I asked why they didn't do something about it, but he said that at her age the only thing they can do is give her a minimal amount of medication to try and bring down the pressure on her brain."

"So, she won't get any better?" Katie heard the tears in her voice.

"Dr. Pelson said if the pressure goes down before too much damage is done, she could regain quite a bit of mobility and brain function, as long as she doesn't have another stroke. What I don't see is how she can take care of herself in that house, and neither you nor any other caretaker could manage to fit in there with her."

Katie sighed. "I guess we'll have to tell her soon, and decide what to do about the house. Even if she can go back to it after she recovers this time, there is no telling how long before she has another episode."

"I need to find out as much as I can about Nana's finances before we talk with her attorney tomorrow," Robert said.

"We can do that now," Katie said. "I've gone through everything from her desk and done a lot of cleaning out, but you should probably review all of that, since you're the accountant, and we should search to see if she has any other places where she might have stashed important papers."

They returned to Nana's room and told her they would be back later, though they weren't sure if she heard them.

Tiff joined them in the lobby and they drove their separate cars to Nana's house.

The three of them walked in together. Katie stopped.

"What is it?" Robert asked, tensing as if ready to fight.

"Nothing I can put my finger on," Katie said. "But I think someone has been in here while I was gone. Yes, I know for sure I put Nana's mail from yesterday on the corner of her desk. Now it is in the center."

Robert relaxed and gave her a skeptical look. "How can you be so certain?"

"Because I'm somewhat OCD," she said. "That was one of my problems at the law firm. I stressed about every little thing. But it happens because I notice every little thing."

Tiff was hanging back, twirling a strand of hair. "Is that all? Maybe someone planted another bomb?"

Robert and Katie went swiftly through the house and found nothing else Katie could determine for sure was different from when she left in the morning, but she was certain about the mail.

Robert still looked skeptical. "Why would they look through Nana's mail? She has nothing to do with Tiff or the case against her."

"Fishing trip," Katie said. "I am connected to Tiff now, so whoever is doing this is gathering all the information they can on both of us and our movements. But Chief Browning would only laugh if I brought it to his attention, so let's go on with our search."

Robert started at the desk, going through the paperwork Katie had sorted and making notes on a pad. Katie went into the room designated a dressing room and found it full of Nano's clothing as well as Nana's. She opened a closet and shook her head. Why had Nana moved all Nano's stuff here, and how did Nana find anything in a closet so fully stuffed?

"Robert," she said, her voice strained.

"What?"

"All of Nano's clothes are here. Nana didn't get rid of anything, even though she moved. Do you think it would upset her too much if I cleared it out?"

"It's hard to know, and hard to know if she'll ever be well enough to care. Let's box it up, maybe get a storage locker somewhere, and wait to see what happens."

Tiff went to the U-Haul store and purchased some boxes. Katie took Nano's clothing out of the closet, checked each piece for anything overlooked in the pockets, and handed it to Tiff to fold into the boxes.

"This is so hard," she said. "I can see why Nana didn't do it." She held up a plaid sports coat. "I remember him wearing this to a school event of mine. I was so embarrassed. There are a lot of memories in this closet."

After the closet was cleared of her grandfather's clothing, Katie started on the chest of drawers. Any of Nano's clothing from the drawers went into bags for a local thrift shop. She was sure Nana wouldn't miss those items.

"Whoa," she said, reaching the bottom of a drawer containing pajamas and t-shirts. "What is this?" She pulled out a cardboard box, the kind designed to hold a ream of paper.

Robert had finished going through the paperwork at the desk, so he came to see what Katie had discovered. "This looks like the arrangements he made before he died, to take care of Nana as long as she lived and to dispose of his assets after she is gone," Katie said, looking through the box. "I wonder if Nana ever looked in the box." She pulled out a sheet of paper. "Here is the trust agreement Mrs. Andrews told us about. And here is a document he signed and had witnessed later, stating that after Nana is gone, the money should be donated to a foundation that funds scholarships to Arizona colleges and universities. He doesn't specify what foundation."

She looked up at Robert, perplexed. "This is dated

after the trust document Mrs. Andrews has. In this one, he doesn't leave anything to us."

Robert was reading another document from the box. "He left a note to us. It says that since he helped Dad fund our college educations, and he believed that those educations would make us able to lead good lives without further help, he wanted to give that opportunity to other young people who might not have the resources to go to college. He hoped we would understand."

Katie wiped a tear from her eye. "That is so like him," she said. "It's a surprise, but I feel good that our inheritance will be used that way."

Robert gave her a hug.

She started replacing the papers in the box. "We have to take this to Mrs. Andrews when we see her. I don't know why, but it looks as if Nano never told either her or Nana about it. I would bet Nana never looked in this box. Now, let's finish with the packing and get some lunch before going to look at that house Marta told us about."

"How do you feel about going to the ZigZag Café?" Katie asked Tiff as they headed out to Robert's rental car.

Tiff shuddered. "Not great. But if I'm going to be around here for a while, I think I'd better get over it."

––––––––––

"Greg," Katie exclaimed when they walked in. "I thought you only worked nights."

"I fill in sometimes when I don't have a class." He looked at Tiff when he added, "I'm glad to see you aren't afraid to come back."

"Have you remembered anything else about that night?" Katie asked.

"Not really. Only that Mr. and Mrs. Wells seemed like such a happy couple." He glanced at Tiff. "I never could believe you did it."

"Have the police talked with you?" Katie asked.

"Yes, but Chief Browning didn't seem to put much credence on the idea that the murderer could have known they were here and contrived to get poison in only one salad that way. Mrs. Wells' attorney, Mr. Leighton, was more interested, but I couldn't give him any more information than I gave you, so I don't think there is anything he can do about it."

The Western Salad Katie had before had been so good Katie decided to try a bacon and avocado salad today. Tiff said she might never eat a salad there again, so she ordered soup, while Robert declared that, since he was already so far off his regular diet, he would splurge on a Reuben.

"What are you going to do now?" Katie asked Robert when they had finished eating.

"I want to spend some time with Nana, but she probably won't even know I'm there, so I think I'll go with you to look at the house."

Katie grinned. "Still protecting me, big brother?"

He looked down at her with a superior air. "Always, little sister."

As much as Katie liked to consider herself

independent and fearless, it made her feel good to have Robert go with them today. The three of them got into Robert's rental car and headed to the address Marta had given them.

The house was on a dirt road that led north from town and curved around a couple of hills. As they drove up to it, a tall, broad-shouldered man came out to greet them.

"Wow! No wonder Marta's so hot about this guy," Tiff whispered to Katie as they got out of the car.

"Welcome," the man said with a toothy smile. "My name is Fred Boyson." His close-cropped light-brown hair added to the rest of his appearance and made Katie think of the former athletes turned salesmen she often saw in television ads.

Fred took her hand in both of his for a moment, did the same with Tiff, and greeted Robert with a firm, manly shake.

"Let me show you around," Fred said, leading them into the house. "This place is tailor-made for two people, with what are essentially two master bedrooms separated by a spacious common area."

Tiff's face was shining as she looked around the great room that separated the bedrooms, expanding into a kitchen at the far end. Robert's expression was closed. He studied the man more than the house. Katie had a hard time concentrating on the house herself. Fred's looks were distracting, but he also seemed too smooth. She shook her head, experiencing a reluctance to trust, as she did with many successful salespeople. That made her guess Fred sold cars or life insurance.

Fred had papers ready and seemed to think it was a done deal that they would rent the house.

"We'll talk about it and get back to you," Katie said while Robert nudged Tiff, who began to look petulant, back out to the car.

"It's perfect," Tiff exclaimed as they drove away. "And the rent is not bad, either. I don't understand why you didn't want to grab it before someone else does."

"Because I don't trust that man. He's too slick."

"Good for you," Robert said. "I was afraid he would charm you both. I didn't like him either."

"Well, I like him, and I like the house, and I think I want to live here while I have to be in Cactus City."

Katie sighed. It would be useless to argue. She elected to change the subject. "Tiff, what do you want to do now? Robert and I will be going to the clinic to spend time with Nana."

While her lower lip still stuck out a little, Tiff seemed resigned to their decision. "I think the little one and I need to rest for a while. May I meet you later?"

"We'll probably be going to the Top View Bar to let Marta know."

Tiff got in her car at Nana's house. As Robert started driving toward the clinic, he glanced in the rearview mirror and frowned. "Where do you suppose she's going now?"

Katie turned around to see Tiff following them. The motel was in the opposite direction. When Robert turned on the street to the clinic, Tiff kept going. She was headed in the direction they had just come from.

CHAPTER SEVENTEEN

Nana's condition had not changed. "She gets a little restless and seems to be becoming more aware, but then sinks back into the coma," the nurse told them.

Katie and Robert arranged chairs on opposite sides of Nana's bed. They took turns relating things from their memories and hopes for their futures. Eventually Katie started to softly sing the hymns she could remember from their childhood. Robert joined in.

"I don't think I can leave tomorrow," Robert said when they left Nana's room. "I'll call the office and ask for more time off."

Katie felt a weight lift. Knowing Robert was here to share this time with her would make the waiting so much easier.

Leaving the clinic, they drove in silence to the Switch Back Motel and picked up Tiff to go to the Top View Bar. Katie bit her tongue to keep from questioning Tiff about where she had gone.

They had hardly arrived at the bar when Marta came swooping over. "So? Did you like the house? Isn't Fred the greatest ever?"

"Oh, Marta, he is such a hunk! You are so lucky that he took to you." Tiff gushed. She seemed unaware of her slight accent on the word "you."

Marta's face lost a little of its glow.

"And, he is lucky that you took to him," Katie added quickly.

Marta gave Tiff a sideways look before turning back to Katie. "So, are you going to rent the house?" she asked.

"I don't know," Katie said. She was reluctant to deal with someone she wasn't sure she trusted, but it would be impossible to find a better deal in Cactus.

"Well, I'm going to," Tiff declared. "Freddie thinks I should be able to take it for a little while, and if Mr. Morley gets some of my money for me, I can keep it as long as I have to be here. Maybe you can help me convince Katie to join me."

"I haven't ruled it out," Katie hastened to add. So, Tiff had returned to the house after we dropped her off. "I'd like to know more about Fred before doing business with him, that's all."

Marta brightened. "I'm sure that's possible. Why don't we all get together before he has to go back to Phoenix?"

"What does he do for a living?" Katie asked.

"He sells insurance."

Of course. "Do you know what company he works with?"

Marta shook her head. "No, I never asked him. But he looks as though he's doing well."

Once they put that discussion behind them, Katie found it easy to relax into the rest of the evening, talking, eating, drinking. She looked at Robert and remembered the times they had shared in the past. She knew they would be less frequent now that she had moved from the Seattle area. Perhaps that was a good thing, since they often did get on each other's nerves. She looked at Tiff. She wasn't sure how she felt about being the person Tiff seemed to need to help her through the challenges that were in store for her.

Freddie? Had Tiff actually rented that house this afternoon?

One more bourbon seemed to bring everything into focus.

A huge headache accompanied Katie's awakening the next morning. She couldn't remember drinking enough to cause it. She couldn't imagine Robert allowing her to drink enough to cause it. Or perhaps she had relied on Robert's overbearing big-brother instincts to protect her and he had decided it was time for her to take care of herself. She was glad she hadn't brought any of the uppers that had become a constant part of her life the last few months in Seattle. It would have been hard to resist the temptation to take one now.

She'd have to get moving without that kind of help. They had an eight o'clock appointment with

Mrs. Andrews. Once she had managed to shower, she felt as if she might eventually be able to handle the day. It hadn't happened yet when and she walked into Mrs. Andrews' office with Robert.

"I know my grandmother didn't have a chance to sign the documents you prepared," Robert was saying when Katie made herself zero in on the conversation. "What can we do to make sure that Kate will be able to handle whatever decisions are necessary in the future?"

"Unfortunately, if your grandmother is unable to complete the paperwork, conservatorship will have to be awarded by the court. Was she able to give a health power of attorney when she went to the clinic?"

"Yes, the first time she went she was able to do that. She gave me the power of attorney," Katie said.

"That's good." Mrs. Andrews finished examining the documents they had brought and folded her hands on her desk. "So, it seems neither of you will benefit from your grandfather's estate when your grandmother dies."

"We both are totally in favor of my grandfather's decision about the disposition of his estate," Robert said. "However, we need to make sure Kate can take proper care of our grandmother."

The attorney's eyes narrowed. "You realize that if your sister is given conservatorship and your grandmother is declared unable to handle her own affairs, your sister can do whatever she wishes with that estate as long as your grandmother is alive?"

Robert's voice was so cold Katie shivered. "I trust my sister completely."

"Do you know the size of the estate we are talking about?" Mrs. Andrews asked.

"Yes, I do."

Katie's head jerked around to look at Robert, causing a shock wave of pain.

"I'm sorry I didn't tell you," he said. "I was too surprised to say anything when I found the latest trust statement stuck in the back of a desk drawer. When you found that box containing the addendum and the note to us it slipped my mind that you didn't know. Because Nana never used much of the money, and Nano invested it well, her estate is now over a million and a half."

Katie felt a huge smile spread across her face. "If that is well managed, what a lot of scholarships it will provide. What a wonderful legacy to leave."

Mrs. Andrews studied Katie a moment with narrowed eyes. "I'll be keeping a close eye on your grandmother's affairs," she said.

"What a dragon," Robert said when they left her office. "But, I guess if there were any question about motives, we'd want her on our side."

Robert, Katie, and Tiff went to Wendy's for breakfast. They had finished eating and were walking out the door of the restaurant when Tiff's phone rang.

"Yes, Mr. Morley," she said, putting the call on speaker as they climbed into Robert's car. "We do have some questions for you."

"First, I have some information for you," Mr. Morley said. "A man who said he was sent by the Build Them Up Foundation, which is evidently the organization Mr. Wells wrote to your husband about, was at my office when I arrived this morning. He gave me a brochure about the organization, which says it was established to provide scholarships to low-income students. He also gave me a copy of the signed and witnessed addendum to Jim Wells' trust that gives the remainder of his estate, after the bequests to Jeffrey, Lila, and Phil, to the foundation outright. If any of those three aren't able to collect their share, it goes to the foundation."

Robert started the car and exited the Wendy's parking lot.

"How large is Dad's estate?" Tiff asked.

"It comes to something over seven million dollars before taxes," Mr. Morley said.

Tiff gasped and nearly dropped her phone. "I had no idea it was so much. So, since this addendum appears to be valid, how much are the bequests to Jeffrey, Lila, and me?"

"As Mr. Wells stated in his letter to your husband, a million and a half each for you and Jeffrey and a million for Lila, to which she agreed in a prenuptial agreement. Leaving three million to the foundation. Minus taxes, of course."

Tiff appeared unable to reply. Katie took the phone from her as Robert pulled into Nana's driveway. "This is Tiffany's friend Kate Christensen," she said. "Tiff appears to be overwhelmed by that news. However, she is in need of money to live on until everything is settled. Does she have access to her benefit now, or is it frozen while the murders are being investigated?"

"As far as I know, she hasn't been charged with murder; so, as his trustee, I'm working on sorting out Mr. Wells' accounts. As soon as possible we'll set up an account at a Cactus City bank, if Tiffany is still there, and transfer some funds into it. I can't guarantee it, though. The authorities may try to get a judge to put a hold on disbursement."

"Do you have any more information on the Build Them Up Foundation?" Katie asked.

"No. I haven't had time to do any investigating, but you can be sure I will."

Katie sat in thought after disconnecting and handing Tiff her phone. "If that organization is set to get close to three million, would they take the risk of killing two people and trying to put the blame on Tiff to get Tiff's share?"

"I wouldn't be surprised," Robert said. "In my accounting work, I come across financial shenanigans that would amaze you. I suspect this group is in the business of defrauding old people and realized they had hit the motherlode. Scam artists don't usually resort to violence, but that is a tempting chunk of money."

"I wonder if Jeffrey was mentioned in the original trust," Katie said. "It seems someone tried to take Jeffrey out of the picture later, as if they didn't know about his share before. But, I don't understand how whoever is doing this knew Tiff and Phil would be eating at the ZigZag Café. Jeffrey could have guessed they would stop there, but no one else even knew they were on their way to Phoenix. And, even Jeffrey didn't know Tiff was going to go see Mr. Wells the day he was killed."

"As far as we know," Robert added.

Katie frowned. Did Jeffrey know how large his uncle's estate was? But the way this change to the trust was written, neither Jeffrey nor Lila gained anything by killing Phil.

Unable to find an explanation for any of this, Katie picked up her phone and called the auto repair shop to see if they were ready to change the tire. "We can go in right now," she said when she disconnected. "The old tire was toast, so they'll put on a new one."

"Is someone keeping track of you?" the mechanic asked when he had finished changing the tire.

"Not that I know of. Why?"

He held up a small, round object. "I found this in the wheel well."

"What is it?" Katie asked, reaching out her hand.

"It looks like a tracking device to me."

Katie pulled her hand back quickly. "Don't give it to me," she said, grabbing her phone. "Give it to the police and show them exactly where you found it."

Since the garage was only three blocks from the police station, Chief Browning arrived quickly, puffing from the short walk. The mechanic explained and showed the chief where he found the device. The chief stood straight, thumbs notched in his belt, and glared at Katie. "Now I need to check Tiffany Wells' car," he said.

Of course, Katie thought. If they were tracking her, she was sure they would find a tracking device on Tiff's car too.

She eyed Robert's rental car. Chances were small, but ... She looked at the mechanic. "Could you check Robert's car while we're here?" she asked.

"You're stretching now," Chief Browning sneered.

The mechanic checked each tire well. On the third one, he stood up holding a small, round device like the one from Katie's car.

"Wow," Katie whispered. "Whoever is doing this really moves fast."

CHAPTER EIGHTEEN

Chief Browning waited at the garage while Robert drove Tiff to the motel to get her car. The mechanic found a tracking device in one of her wheel wells.

"I hope you'll now rethink your assumption that Tiff is the bad guy here," Katie said, turning to the chief.

"Hmmph," he replied. "Anyone could plant those devices to throw us off track. And that includes Mrs. Tiffany Wells."

"He's right, Robert," Katie said when Chief Browning had stomped back to the police station. "Tiff was planning to drive to Prescott to register at a modeling agency. After finding these tracking devices, I don't think she should go right now."

"Why, so they'll have time to plant some more?" Tiff asked. "I think right now is the safest time to go."

Unfortunately, this was one of those rare times when Tiff made good sense.

"Why can't we both go with her?" Robert asked.

"We'll still be able to see Nana when we get back. And I don't think either of you should be going anywhere alone, especially on treacherous mountain roads."

Robert insisted on driving, of course. Katie had started to argue, but realized it made no difference who drove. None of them had much experience on switchbacks like these; the ones in Washington state weren't nearly as sharp. In fact, Robert's extra strength might help keep them safe if something did happen.

She was glad she wasn't the one driving when they hit the hairpin curves. She had driven through them before, at the posted fifteen and twenty miles an hour, but she had not been able to enjoy the expansive views that opened up each time they rounded a curve.

Paranoid about the possibility of being followed, she glanced frequently over her shoulder. Still, she wasn't prepared for the car that loomed behind them on a sharp curve around a mountain on the right. Robert slowed when it pulled out and started to pass. Barely halfway past, it began to swerve back into their lane. Robert wrenched the steering wheel hard to the right, then back to the left before they slammed into the side of the mountain. Tiff's scream was still echoing when the motor died. The other car disappeared around the curve ahead of them.

No one moved for a moment "Is everyone all right?" Robert finally asked and started to get out of the car.

"Don't open the door!" Katie cried. Robert barely got it pulled back in before another car came speeding around the mountain from behind, narrowly missing them.

"Will the car start?" Katie asked. "Cars coming around that curve can't see us. We need to get off this narrow shoulder onto a pull-off before someone hits us."

Fortunately, the motor turned over. Robert backed onto the road and quickly shifted to drive before another vehicle could come sailing up behind them. Around two more bends they found a pull-over so they could get off the road and take stock.

Katie finally turned around to look at Tiff, who hadn't muttered another sound after the scream. Her normal tan was waxy looking, her face pinched.

"Was that on purpose?" Tiff asked, her voice thin.

"It looked like it, but people drive so crazy on these curves it's hard to be sure. Are you all right?"

Tiff nodded. "What if I'd been by myself? I don't think I could have controlled the car."

Katie looked at Robert. "That was a pretty nifty move. We would have hit a lot harder if you hadn't turned back to the left."

"Thanks," Robert said with a wry grin, carefully stepping out of the car to assess the damage. "Not as bad as it could have been," he said when he returned, "but enough for the rental agency to be unhappy." His mouth was set in a grim line. "I wish I'd been able to get a good look at the driver, or even the car. I have no idea what make or model it was, only that it was white."

Katie shook her head. "Why push us into the side of the mountain?" she asked. "If it was deliberate, why not find a way to force us off the road on the other side? That would probably send us over the edge." She thought about it for a moment. "I don't think they were trying to kill us."

"You could have fooled me," Robert said.

"Like that explosion, placed where it could hurt but most likely not kill. And I didn't think they could have known Tiff was pregnant yet—but, after finding those tracking devices on all of our cars, I'm not sure what they might know. They may be trying to make her miscarry." She paused. "Those tracking devices might also give us a clue as to how whoever is doing this knew Phil and Tiff stopped at the café."

"Wow," Robert said. "There's a whole lot of conjecture in there, but it also makes a weird kind of sense."

"Let's go back to the motel," Tiff said, her voice still weak.

Katie was shaking her head even before she thought it through. "No, we're over halfway there, and I don't think they'll try anything again this trip. We'll have lunch in Prescott, unwind, and you can check in with the modeling agency. And maybe we'll introduce ourselves at the temporary work agencies."

"I don't even need to look for work," Tiff said. "Not if Mr. Morley can get my money released."

"That's a big if," Katie said. "I think he'll do it, but we don't know how long it will take. And, as Mr. Leighton said, if it comes to trial, it will look better for you that you have found a job rather than relying on an inheritance."

"Well, I'm not driving back without some food in my stomach, anyway," Robert said. "I seem to recall there are some good restaurants in Prescott." He pulled back out on the road and within a few minutes they exited the switchbacks and drove to Route 69 on a relatively quiet highway.

After a hearty lunch at Prescott Junction, Tiff looked strong enough to handle the rest of the afternoon. They stopped by the modeling agency, where she put in her application and spoke with the agent.

"She said they won't have any trouble finding jobs for me, though they don't have any right now," Tiff said. "She seemed impressed with my credentials."

Katie took a look at her new friend. Could Tiff really not know how perfectly she looked the part of a fashion model? Especially dressed as she was now in fitted, washed-out jeans and a crisp, white, tailored blouse unbuttoned to the third button. Even the slight scars on her face, healing fast, added to her allure.

Their welcome at the two temporary agencies was less enthusiastic. "You just put in your application," one case manager said. "We have many people ahead of you on our list. When a job isn't filled by someone ahead of you, we will call you."

The person at the other agency said basically the same thing.

Katie's mind was working in overdrive to find another avenue to employment as they drove back to Cactus City. It wouldn't stay focused, though. She frowned. "If whoever is threatening us knows Tiff is pregnant, the main thing they have to do now is make Tiff miscarry. Until that happens, until Phil doesn't have an heir, it won't make any difference for them if she is convicted or not."

"Oh, my God," Tiff exclaimed. "Maybe I should leave town. Maybe I should go to Mexico and let them have the money. They took everyone I loved. I can't let them kill my baby too."

"I hope you don't have to do anything so drastic. Why don't we see if Mr. Leighton has any ideas on how to keep you safe?" Katie asked. "Why don't you call him now and let him know what happened and what we think it means?"

Robert and Katie remained silent while Tiff talked with Mr. Leighton, her phone on speaker. He was concerned about the incident on the road. He said they could find a house for her, but if she was being so closely observed it might be hard to be sure she would be safe once she was in it. If it did work, she wouldn't be able to leave for any reason without jeopardizing her safety. That would be impossible if either the Cactus City police or the Phoenix police required her presence.

By the time they arrived in Cactus City, they were thoroughly confused about what to do next and how to protect Tiff.

First, they stopped by the clinic so Robert and Katie could check on Nana. Her condition was unchanged.

They spent a little time there, talking to her, letting her know they loved her, anything they could think to help her.

The nurse in charge was not encouraging. "The longer she stays in this state, the less likely it is that she'll recover," she said. "You definitely should be looking at the possibility of long-term care."

"Well, at least we know she can afford it," Katie said when they left.

"At the expense of Nano's legacy," Robert said.

Katie stared at him. "Surely Nana's care comes first."

"Of course, it does. Only, it would be such a shame if her care took all of the money he had hoped to leave to such a worthy cause."

Tiff had been waiting for them in the foyer, afraid to wait alone in the car.

"I think I'm ready to go to the Top View and relax a bit," Katie said.

Robert gave her a sidelong look. "You would be," he said.

"What's that supposed to mean?" Katie snapped.

"You ran away from substance abuse in Seattle. Are you going to fall right back into the pattern here?"

"You have no idea the substances that were being abused in my firm in Seattle. I didn't run away from my own substance abuse, but from being tempted and pressured into it. Anyway, that wasn't the only problem."

Robert didn't look convinced, but he drove to the bar anyway.

Marta greeted them with her usual high-wattage welcome, a scotch and water for Robert and a double bourbon with a side of water for Katie. She looked at Tiff expectantly. Tiff gave Katie a sideways glance and ordered a tonic water with a twist of lemon.

"And a Nachos Grande for all of us," Katie added.

They had barely begun to relax when the door flew open. Heads around the bar turned when Jeffrey charged in and shouted at Tiff, "What the hell are you trying to do?"

Tiff shrank back. "What do you mean?"

"You are trying to kill me, like you killed Phil and Uncle Jim!"

CHAPTER NINETEEN

"Jeffrey," Katie said, using her best Katherine Ann Christensen attorney voice. "With the size of the benefit she already stands to get, and the fact that the way that addendum is written, she can't gain any more. Why would Tiff try to get rid of you?"

"Addendum?" Jeffrey frowned and shook his head. His voice went down a notch. "Well, someone did it."

"Sit down and talk to us," Katie said, drawing him to their table. "What exactly happened?"

Katie was glad to note that they were no longer the center of attention in the bar. Jeffrey hesitated before he sat down next to Robert with a sigh. "The first time, my brake lines were cut. Fortunately, when I discovered I didn't have brakes I was going slow and there wasn't much traffic. I put the car in neutral and coasted to the side of the road. I was on my way to Cactus City at the time."

"Did you make a report to the police?"

"Of course, I did. That's how I found out where you were staying. But what could they do? By the time I discovered they'd been cut, I had no idea where or when it had been done."

"Where were you coming from and why were you coming to Cactus City?"

"What difference does that make?" Jeffrey tensed and put his hands on the table as if to stand, then deflated. "I have business here. I'm in real estate in Phoenix, and I get clients who want a place in the mountains. I come up to check things out for them. I know them and their needs better than a local agent here would."

"I still don't know why you thought I would, or could, cut your brake lines," Tiff said. "And I still think you are the one who set me up for Phil and Dad's murders. Even though it'll do you no good."

Jeffrey looked confused again.

"What about now? What happened this time?" Katie cut in quickly. "We know Tiff was in the clinic when your brake lines were cut. When did this incident happen?"

Jeffrey hesitated, shot Tiff a puzzled look. "Well, she could have had someone do it for her. She wouldn't have any problem luring men into doing her bidding."

Katie had to put a hand on Tiff's arm to keep her from responding.

"Forget the supposition. What happened? And when?"

"Well, I drove to a knife-throwing competition in

Cottonwood. When I left, I decided to take my car to a mechanic to make sure the brakes would work on the drive back down. The mechanic found little devices on my tires that would explode at a certain speed." He glared at Tiffany.

"Tiffany has been with Robert and me all day, hasn't she, Robert?" Katie asked. At his nod, she turned back to Jeffrey. "How would she even know where you were?"

Jeffrey shook his head. "How would anyone else? And who else would have a motive?"

"That's what we're trying to figure out," Katie said. "How much do you know about your uncle's trust?"

"Not much," he said. "I knew he was wealthy, but he had no reason to leave me anything. I guess he did leave me something, though, because Mr. Morley asked me to come see him tomorrow."

"He was probably a lot wealthier than you imagine," Katie said. "But a group called the Build Them Up Foundation managed to get him to write an addendum to his trust to give it around three million and make it contingent beneficiary for what he left to you and Lila. It will also get Phil's share if he has no heirs who can inherit."

Jeffrey jerked back in his chair, his eyes wide. "That's what I was afraid of," he said. "That's why I tried to take control of his affairs. But, you already know what he left to the three of us?"

"You should probably talk with Mr. Morley about that. I can tell you that the only one who benefits if something happens to either of you is this Build Them Up Foundation. Before leaving town, you should take your car back to the mechanic and have him go over it for tracking devices," she said. "And, we need to get Chief Browning up to speed about what has been happening."

Tiff finally exploded. "Really! You are going to believe this man, who tried to have me convicted of killing Phil and Dad? Who tried to run us off the road today?"

Robert held up his hands. "Wait, wait," he said. "It looks as if neither of you could have personally attacked the other, at least today. You were both busy doing other things. And neither of you gains if the other one dies, even though you didn't know that before. I agree with Kate. There has to be a third party involved."

"I guess I need to talk with Mr. Morley before I understand what you are saying. But, a third party ..." Jeffrey said, his face registering doubt. "Like his new wife? Or this Build Them Up Foundation?"

"Exactly," Katie said. "Although Lila doesn't get any more if something happens to one of you either."

"I was beginning to worry about Uncle Jim's abilities, but he must have checked out this foundation. He was too good a businessman to be taken in by charlatans," Jeffrey said. "I think Lila is a gold digger. Maybe she decided what he left her wasn't enough and thought she could get her hands on more."

Katie shook her head, deciding she still shouldn't

tell Jeffrey anything more. "He was getting older. He knew he had more money than Phil and you would need. He was probably eager to find a way to use his money to do some good. And what is better than scholarships to open up education to more young people? My own grandfather did that. Mr. Wells may have been easy to convince."

Jeffrey looked at Tiff, his face still registering disbelief. "So, you really are not trying to get me out of the way?"

Tiff snorted, startling Katie. "With what Dad left me? Why would I take a chance like that? But, I'll bet you wanted more, so you needed me out of the way."

"Uh, why?" Katie interjected. "Don't forget Jeffrey won't get anything more even if you are convicted of the murders. It'll go to your child. Which is why I think we need to be looking more closely at the foundation."

"Your child?" Jeffrey exclaimed. Understanding seemed to dawn on his face. "That's why you said it would do me no good?"

Jeffrey and Tiff stared at each other, their expressions guarded.

"Let's get Jeffrey's car over to the garage and inform Chief Browning what is going on," Robert suggested. "And while we're there, we can have them check my rental again." They all agreed to that.

Chief Browning arrived at the garage while the mechanic was inspecting the trunk of Jeffrey's car. "Now what are you up to?" he demanded.

Before anyone could answer, the mechanic emerged from the trunk with two of the small tracking devices in his hand. Smart, Katie thought. They put the tracking devices where they wouldn't be spotted when the mechanics were working on the other problems.

"Someone must have bought these things wholesale," the mechanic said.

"So, someone is tracking all of you," Chief Browning said. "Are you sure you're not working some devious plot together?"

"I think someone is trying to pit these two against each other, while making Tiff look guilty of murder, in order to get their hands on the rest of Mr. Wells' estate," Katie said.

The police chief glared at each one of them in turn. "All right. I think I need to interview you all again. You seem to have information you have not seen fit to tell me."

Katie's hands balled into fists. "Can it wait until tomorrow? My brother and I have enough on our plates right now trying to figure out what to do about our grandmother's situation."

Much to her surprise, Chief Browning agreed. "I'd like to get home for dinner. If one of you isn't going to kill the other off tonight, we're probably safe for now."

––––––––––

"Oh good, you're back," Marta said when they returned to the Top View. She looked back and forth between Tiff and Jeffrey. "So, is everything okay with you now?"

Tiff shrugged. Jeffrey didn't respond.

"Let me get you some fresh drinks." She turned to Jeffrey. "What would you like?"

"I have to get back down the mountain. I have an early appointment with a client tomorrow." He turned to Katie. "If Chief Browning really needs to talk with me, he can get in touch with me tomorrow. It appears I don't know the information he wants to get from you, so he may not need me."

"Could you stay for a few more minutes?" Katie asked. "I think we need to compare notes before you leave."

He agreed and asked Marta for a cup of coffee. Marta left them at their table and returned with their drinks and a platter of Nachos Grande. Katie took a healthy swig of her bourbon before adding water.

"What?" she said at Robert's look.

He shook his head.

Marta walked over to their table. "May I intrude for a minute?" she asked.

"You are always welcome," Katie said.

"I wanted to let you know Fred agrees you should get to know him better, and vice versa, before proceeding with renting the house. He has not taken the lease Tiff signed to the owner yet. He would like to meet with both of you, at your convenience, to make sure everything is satisfactory."

Katie hesitated, started to look at Robert for

guidance, and quickly averted her gaze. She was a successful corporate attorney. She didn't need her big brother to make decisions for her. She and Tiff did need a place to live, and that house was as close to perfect as they could find. If only she felt she could trust Fred.

"Have him get in touch with Tiff or me directly," she said. "You shouldn't be a go-between."

It occurred to her that she should probably ask to meet the owner of the house that had so conveniently become available. But that would have to wait for now. She didn't want to spoil the mood when Marta's smile lit up the room.

"All right, Jeffrey," Katie said when they were settled with their drinks. "I understand you were trying to take control of your uncle's affairs before Phil and Tiff arrived. What was that all about?"

"Pretty much what did happen," he said. "I could tell Uncle Jim was starting to lose his sharpness, and I was afraid someone would take advantage of him, especially when I found out that Lila character was planning a wedding. Phil was busy with his own life and hadn't paid much attention to his father for years." He looked at Tiff. "When Phil was poisoned, I couldn't see how it could have been anyone but you." He scowled. "I still don't know how else it could have happened. And they did find that poison in your car."

"They found the poison in the car *later*," Tiff said. "I hadn't gone near our car since we checked in at the motel and went to the café. Why would I keep some of the poison used to kill him in the car? But why didn't you get in touch with Phil about Dad's condition?"

Jeffrey shrugged, looked uncomfortable. "I wasn't trying to cheat Phil. He never seemed interested in his father's welfare, and I thought that if I took good care of Uncle Jim he might leave me something." He looked up, the belligerence returning to his face. "I believe the only reason Phil decided to come now was to protect his interest in the estate."

Tiff visibly bristled at that, but the changed tone of the conversation made Katie hope they could get past their animosity and concentrate on the problem they both faced. "I think whoever is trying to pit you two against each other will soon learn they have failed, if they haven't already. Since they've managed to stay under the radar so far, they could sit back now and wait to see how the investigations develop and, rather than take any more risks, settle for their part of the estate."

"You think that after killing twice to get the whole thing, they will give up now?" Robert asked.

"Unlikely," Jeffrey said. "Another scenario might be that they give up trying to put the blame on Tiff. They could try to get rid of Tiff and the baby. If they aren't caught, they get her share too."

"If they do that," Katie said, "they'll probably try to rig it to make you look guilty in order to stay out of the picture themselves. In that case, they might also get your share."

Jeffrey looked a little pale when he rose to leave.

CHAPTER TWENTY

The nachos spoiled their appetites for dinner, so they decided to call it a day. Robert dropped Katie off at Nana's house before taking Tiff back to the motel.

Katie was ready for a drink. She had been too aware of Robert's disapproving eye at the bar, and had been wanting another drink for over an hour. In fact, right now she could use one of those downers she had grown accustomed to in Seattle. She had flushed them down the toilet before she left, however, so she would have to settle for bourbon.

Sipping her drink, Katie paced the two steps back and forth she could manage in the tiny living room. She wanted to find out more about the Build Them Up Foundation. She was becoming convinced that the people behind it were the murderers. She also wanted to see what she could discover about Fred Boyson. She couldn't do either at Nana's house. Tomorrow she would have to figure out how to get Wi-Fi service.

Keyed up about the events of the day, Katie knew sleep wouldn't come soon. She turned off the inside lights and stepped outside to have more room to pace. She stopped and stared into the darkness. In the moonlight, she could see someone kneeling by the trunk of her car. Someone slight of build, with a floppy brimmed hat covering his head and face. She was sure it was the same person who had been trying to plant evidence in the rental unit.

As if sensing her presence, he scooted around behind the car. Katie reached down, but all she could find were the small stones that made up the driveway. Grabbing a fistful of them, she quietly walked to the side of the car. When she peeked over, he rose and sprinted away. She threw her handful of stones at him as she took up the chase.

When he raised his arms to ward off the stones, she saw the bandage on his right wrist. It was the same person. She picked up speed as he entered the street and had nearly caught up to him when a car careened around a corner behind her and came directly at her. She jumped to the side of the street, falling backward in her effort to avoid it. The car slowed enough for the other person to jump in before it sped away.

She got to her feet, shaking. Was that the same car that had run them off the road going to Prescott? The only thing she could tell for sure, in the dark, was that it was a white sedan. She brushed sand and gravel from her knees and hands and limped to the house to get her phone and call the police station.

"You want someone to do what?"

"Check my car for tracking devices. You don't need to bother Chief Browning about it tonight, but he'll want to know if the intruder placed some new ones in my car."

A few minutes later, a patrol car arrived. The young officer from the night of Phil's death checked under the wheel well on the right side of the trunk, where Katie had seen the man. He found a tracking device.

"I guess I'd better check the other three wheels," he said.

"If you think you need to," Katie said. "But he must have arrived after I got home or I would have seen him sooner, which doesn't give him much time for planting them, and it only takes one to keep tabs on a vehicle. However, I think Tiffany Wells' car and my brother Robert's rental car, both parked at the Switch Back Motel, should be checked first thing in the morning."

The officer agreed, told Katie he'd leave a report on the chief's desk, and left.

Whether it was the extra exertion or the bourbon catching up with her, when she went back into Nana's house she dropped onto the bed and fell into a deep sleep that lasted until six in the morning.

Dragging herself out of bed, Katie showered and pulled on jeans and a knit shirt. She poured a cup of coffee and sat down at Nana's desk. She frowned, remembering the envelopes that she was sure had been moved. That, along with all those tracking devices they had found, should have made her realize that whoever had come into Nana's house might have planted something here too. She was relieved Chief Browning wasn't in when she called, but the young detective was. She asked him to come back again.

"Listening devices," he said, showing her a fistful of them after inspecting the house. "These people really want to keep tabs on you."

It was too early to call Robert, but she wanted to get on the Internet and start looking for information on the Build Them Up Foundation. Grabbing her laptop, she took off for Wendy's, grateful that they were open early. Fifteen minutes later, she sat at a table with an egg burrito, orange juice, and another cup of coffee in front of her.

Booting up her laptop, she ran a search on the foundation. The search engine found nothing. Mr. Morley hadn't seemed to doubt it was a real organization. As soon as it was office hours, she would call and find out what he had learned about it.

Next, she searched for Fred Boyson. There were several hits on his name: one with the announcement that he had joined the Valley Insurance Company, another when he was named Salesperson of the Year, and yet another announcing his marriage. Oh, no. Marta was going to be heartbroken. Katie stared at the photo with the wedding announcement. Fred had his arm protectively around an athletic-looking woman. Frowning, Katie copied the photo to a file on her computer. Was she sure the person she had seen last night and at the rental was a man?

She must be too wound up. She had no reason to think Fred was involved just because she didn't particularly like him, and the wedding announcement was from five years ago, so he might no longer be married. She didn't need to pass up on renting the house because she didn't like the man. It didn't even belong to him.

Her phone rang. Robert informed her he was up and ready for the day. "Should I knock on Tiff's door to see if she wants to join us?"

"No, I think this is still too early for her. If she doesn't call us by about ten, we can check and see what she's doing. I'm at Wendy's. Do you want to come here for breakfast before we visit Nana?"

Robert agreed. A few minutes later, he sat across from her with a scrambled egg breakfast.

"Do you know why the police were checking my car again this morning?" he asked.

She told him about her adventure last night and the listening devices found this morning.

"You what?!" Heads turned at his startled remark. He lowered his voice as he continued. "That man could have had a weapon. You could have been killed."

Katie shrugged off his concern and, to distract him, told him what her Internet search had turned up on Fred Boyson.

"I agree not liking him isn't a good reason to pass

on the house, but I think it's more than that," Robert said. "You've already caught him in a possible lie, and I think you suspect him of something more, even if it isn't the murders. Trust your instincts."

Katie thought about that for a minute, conceding that Robert might be right.

They left Wendy's at about ten. Parking her car at Nana's house, Katie joined Robert in the rental car to go to the clinic. Even though they couldn't see any response from Nana, they stayed for about an hour, until the nurse indicated they should let her rest and come back later.

Katie turned back as they were leaving the room and grabbed Robert's arm. She stood in the doorway, afraid to move. Nana's eyes were open, and she was looking at them.

By the time they could react and return to the bed, her eyes were closed again.

"We'll be back later, Nana," Katie promised. "You get some rest now."

"What does that mean?" Robert asked the nurse.

"It's hard to say," she answered. "It might indicate she is becoming more aware but isn't yet able to communicate. If that's the case, you are doing exactly the right thing coming frequently but not staying too long."

"And if that's not the case?" Katie asked.

The nurse hesitated. "If she can hear you, and we tend to believe she can, your presence is a comfort to her whether or not she regains consciousness."

The reality of the situation was a heavy weight on Katie's shoulders. As they left the facility, Robert put a comforting arm around her. "I know you weren't prepared for this when you came here," Robert said. "Quite selfishly, though, I'm glad you're here. I plan to stay the rest of this week, but I'll have to get back to work soon. You know I'll help any way I can."

Katie nodded, unable to speak. Her phone rang. She didn't look at the display when she answered, expecting it to be Tiff.

"So, you had another visitor last night," the police chief barked.

"I had another visit. I suspect it was the same visitor."

"What makes you say that?"

"The size and shape of the person, the floppy hat he was wearing, and a bandage or brace on the wrist where I hit him with a rock the last time. I say him, but from the size and shape, it could be a woman."

Robert's head jerked up.

"You didn't get a good look at the driver or the license plate of the car that you think tried to run you down?"

"No. But I'm pretty sure it was the same car that ran us off the road on the way to Prescott yesterday."

"Say, what? Why am I only hearing about this now?"

"Because there was absolutely nothing we could tell you about the car or the driver. It all happened too fast. By the way, Tiff was in the car when it happened, so I doubt she had anything to do with it."

"I have to go now, but I plan to get back to you about all of this."

When the call ended, Robert turned to Katie. "What makes you think it could have been a woman?"

"It didn't occur to me until I searched for Fred on the Internet and I saw the picture of him and his bride. She is about the right size, and she looked athletic."

"You think Fred is connected to the murders … why?"

Katie shook her head. "I don't know. It's a feeling I need to sort out. Like this Build Them Up Foundation that I can find no records for. I even searched the yellow pages online. Nothing."

Her phone rang again. This time it was Tiff. "Have you eaten?" Katie asked.

"No, I don't feel very hungry."

"I hate to be a nag, Tiff, but you need to watch your nutrition now that you are pregnant. Skipping meals isn't good."

"I have some crackers, which is all I can handle right now. I think I want to stay here and relax until lunchtime."

"All right. Let's meet at noon for lunch at the café."

As soon as that call ended, she dialed Mr. Morley's number. "Have you been able to find anything about the Build Them Up Foundation?" she asked.

"No. When I couldn't find any information, I had my secretary search the Corporation Commission website, but she could find no listing for either a corporation or an LLC by that name. I went through Mr.

Wells' files at his house and found the addendum to his trust. But I did not find any information about the foundation there either."

"You said that a man brought the copy of the addendum to you after Mr. Wells was killed? And a different man brought you the papers about the Build Them Up Foundation?"

"Yes."

"This is a long shot, but could you look up Fred Boyson on the Internet? There is a photo of his wedding a few years ago. I'm wondering if he could possibly have been one of the men."

"I'll do that, and then I'll call you back," Mr. Morley said. He ended the call.

Katie turned back to Robert. "I feel so stuck," she said. "I can't seem to move forward with anything. I need a job; I need a place to live. I'd like to start getting Nana's house ready to sell, but what will she think if she regains her capacity to live there? She might hate me for it."

"I can set your mind at rest about one thing," Robert said. "Nana could never hate you. You were the little girl she never had. That's one of the reasons Mom always avoided her—she seemed to think Nana wanted to take you away from her."

"Oh, no! Don't tell me I'm the reason they never got along."

"No, of course not. It was their problem, not yours. You had no hand in causing it. I'm only saying, Nana adores you and would forgive you for anything."

"So, do you think I should be looking at selling her house?"

"Absolutely. And I'll help you do it. I don't care how far Nana comes back from this stroke, she should not be living in that house. We can't sell the house unless one of us is entrusted to handle her affairs, but we have only cleared out Nano's things. There is a whole lot more we can do under the radar."

Katie stared at him. "Why am I the attorney and you sound like one?"

"Accounting isn't that different. We learn a lot from how people handle their money, which affects their relationships and so much more about their lives."

Mr. Morley called back a few minutes later. "Sorry, no cigar. That doesn't mean this Fred person isn't involved. In fact, I had the distinct impression both people who came to my office were from hired messenger services. People do have to sign in with the receptionist to come into attorney offices, though, so I'll follow up and see what I can find."

"Thank you," Katie said, feeling deflated again. One step forward, two steps back. She shook her head and stood. "Come on, Robert, let's go see what we can do with Nana's house."

Katie and Robert filled their cars with all that remained of their grandfather's personal items, the throw rugs, and the objects Katie had feared would pose a fall threat for their grandmother. They took the items to the Nearly New thrift shop before meeting Tiff for lunch.

Katie's phone rang as they walked from their cars to the café. "This is Fred Boyson. I wonder when we can get together and talk about the house."

Katie wanted to learn more about him before she decided what to do. "We're about to have lunch at the ZigZag Café," she said. "Would you like to join us?"

"I'll be there in five minutes."

Tiff gave a huge smile when Katie told her Fred would be joining them. "So, have you changed your mind about renting the house with me?"

"I haven't made up my mind," Katie said.

Fred's broad shoulders seemed to fill the room when he arrived and strode to the table. He should go into politics, Katie thought. He had a presence that drew attention.

"Mrs. Wells, Ms. Christensen, Mr. Christensen." His full attention shifted to each person as he intoned their names. "I'm so glad you agreed to see me again."

"I'm curious," Katie dove in as soon as they were all seated. "Why are you so eager to rent to us? I'm sure you could find many people who would jump at the deal you are offering."

He bestowed his radiant smile on her. "I feel it was meant to be," he said. "Our needs match up so perfectly. My friend doesn't want a permanent tenant; you don't need a permanent rental. You'll be looking for a suitable situation while she's getting prepared to do the renovations before selling the place."

After the waitress had taken their lunch orders, Fred pulled a sheaf of papers from his briefcase and handed them to Robert. "I know you aren't the one who will be renting it, but I understand you're an accountant. You can look over the rental agreement I've prepared, in case the ladies decide to take the place."

Robert read through the papers. "Everything seems to be in order," he said, handing them to Katie when their food arrived. He looked at Katie and raised his eyebrows as if to tell her the next move was hers.

Since Tiff was going to rent the house no matter what, Katie decided to be more open to the possibility. She noted that Tiff had already signed the lease, along with Taylor Swift as lessor. "I'm a little concerned that we have not met the person who will be our landlord," she hedged. "Would it be possible to do that?"

"She is out of the state on business right now. It may be a while before we can arrange a meeting."

Katie rubbed her brow. "This unusual flexibility does help us. I may have to make other arrangements quickly if my grandmother leaves rehab, but Tiff has already rented the house, regardless of whether or not I join her. So, Tiff, I'll stay with you for now and kick in my half of the rent and other expenses. But, if I decide to leave for any reason, you're on your own." She turned to Fred. "I still think we should meet the landlord as soon as possible, but it looks like you have a deal."

Tiff jumped up and ran around the table, throwing her arms around Katie. "Oh, thank you, thank you!" she cried.

Fred gave a broad smile. "The house is ready for move-in. I've dated the papers for tomorrow so Mrs. Wells doesn't need to spend any more time at the motel."

It was unsettling that Fred was so sure of himself, but Katie had her own motives. Even though she knew it was a stretch, this was the best way to try to find out if Fred might be the slick salesman who helped himself to a good portion of Jim Wells' estate.

They ate for a few minutes in silence before Katie asked, "Say, you work in insurance, right?"

"Yes." Fred seemed to be put on guard.

"You must deal a lot with bequests to charitable organizations."

"Yes, as a matter of fact, that is one of my specialties."

"So," Katie held her breath. She hoped she wasn't playing her hand too soon. "Have you ever heard of the Build Them Up Foundation?"

Fred cocked his head, as if in thought. Katie wondered if the gesture was meant to hide his reaction to her question. If he was involved, he would know they had talked with Mr. Morley and would have heard about the foundation.

"No, I don't think I know that one," he said. "Do you have an interest in it?"

"My grandfather directed that his estate be used for scholarships after my grandmother dies. I heard Mr. Wells left money to that one, and I wondered if it might be a good one to explore for her."

Tiff and Robert stared at Katie as if she had lost her

mind. Maybe she had. She needed to jar something loose somehow, and this was all she could think of.

"I never heard of that organization, but I'd be happy to talk with your grandmother about the possibilities."

Well, if he was in on it he'd sidestepped that gambit easily enough. "She's incapacitated right now. We'll talk to her about it when she is better."

When they finished eating, Fred handed a copy of the lease to Tiff, along with two sets of keys. He stood to leave.

"Will we see you at the Top View this evening?" Tiff asked.

"No, I have to get back to Phoenix now."

"Oh, Marta will be disappointed," Katie said. Marta was going to be disappointed, anyway, unless Fred and the woman in the newspaper photo had since parted ways. But she suspected Fred had achieved what he wanted by courting Marta and she wouldn't be seeing him again.

"Kate, what were you thinking?" Robert asked after Fred left. "If he does have anything to do with this, he is now aware that you are suspicious of the Build Them Up Foundation."

"I know. But we need to do something. Maybe if we push enough buttons something will break loose."

"So, I can move into the house tomorrow?" Tiff squealed.

"I guess you can. That's the date he put on the lease."

For a moment, Katie joined Tiff in elation at having a place with their own decent-sized bedrooms and bathrooms. Then the rest of their problems flooded back into her mind. If Tiff was going to keep the house, she and Katie had to get jobs. Nana needed a place to stay if ... when ... she came out of the clinic, and she would want it to be her own house. Tiff still might be charged with Phil's death, if not his father's. And they had to be watchful for any threats to Tiff's unborn baby.

"I want to go see Nana again," Katie said as they left the restaurant. "What about you, Tiff?"

"The medical examiner has released Phil's body. It's at Morton's Funeral Home, and they have made the arrangements with the one in San Diego to take care of everything. I'm going to Morton's now to order the extra death certificates I need and to find out what I need to do for Phil's final ceremonies."

"Do you need any help?" Katie asked.

"No, I don't think so. The funeral home will handle everything and let me know what I need to do."

"She's a sweet girl, even if she is a bit flaky sometimes," Robert said as they drove to the clinic. "I hope she doesn't get charged with her husband's murder."

When they arrived at Nana's room, they found her with her eyes open and the head raised on her bed. She smiled in greeting.

"Nana!" Katie cried, running to her. "Oh, you look so much better."

"Feel better," Nana whispered. She looked over at Robert. "Knew you were here."

The nurse came into the room with a wide smile on her face. "The swelling from the brain bleed has gone down significantly. Lillian has already made great strides in recovery. We believe she is going to make a lot more. We'll keep her here for another day or two. If she keeps up this progress, Dr. Pelson will probably send her over to the Rest Easy Nursing Home for rehab."

"How long do you think she might be in rehab?" Katie asked the nurse.

"It's hard to know. We have to wait until we get her on her feet before we can assess how much mobility she may have lost."

"And, after rehab?"

"I think the doctor would like to see her go to assisted living. The facilities we have in Cactus City are very pleasant. They offer socialization, nutritious food, entertainment, and appropriate fitness routines to continue the rehab progress."

"That sounds good, doesn't it, Nana?" Katie asked.

"Home." Nana's voice sounded firm.

Katie's heart sank. "We'll talk about it after you are well enough to leave rehab," Katie said, sitting down on one side of the bed.

Robert sat on the other side. "We have been doing all the talking. Now we want to hear from you."

"Heard you," Nana said, a slight sparkle in her eyes.

"That's the best news," Robert said. "And, what do you think about what we talked about?"

"Thought I was dying," she said.

Katie felt a choking at the back of her throat. She couldn't believe the hint of teasing accusation she heard in Nana's voice.

It seemed like no time at all had passed before the nurse indicated they should leave to let Nana rest.

"Robert, we can't sell that house," Katie said as they walked out of the clinic. "I can't do that to Nana. Even if she never goes back to it, it has to be there for her."

"It's too bad you can't live in it," Robert said. "It'll be an extra expense to keep it when you're living somewhere else."

"I'll try to come up with something." She frowned in thought. "I know, I'll check on the zoning. We might be able to find some other use for it."

"I'll leave it up to you," Robert said. "If you decide we should sell it, I'll back you."

"But, right now, we need to see Chief Browning," Katie said.

"Why?" Robert looked confused. Katie grinned. With the relationship she had with Chief Browning, she could understand Robert's question.

"I have a feeling Fred has a reason for wanting us in that house. Our stalker is known for planting tracking devices. If he has anything to do with the house, he probably also planted listening devices there, like he did at Nana's house."

"Now that you have brought up the possibility, I wouldn't be comfortable if you went into the house without checking."

The chief wasn't concerned. "We do not have

unlimited resources to follow up on your whims," he said. "This person being willing to rent to you doesn't make him a suspect."

The young officer who kept turning up interceded. "It won't take any time at all to check it out, Chief. I can do it tomorrow as soon as Mrs. Wells takes possession of the property."

"We keep meeting up, but I never heard your name," Katie said.

"Ken Wilson, Ms. Christensen." He gave her a shy smile.

"What time do you come on duty in the morning?"

"Ten o'clock." He looked at the storm clouds in his superior's eyes. "But I can come there before I start my shift."

"Thank you. Any time after nine will be fine." She glared her own storm clouds at the chief before Robert and she left.

———————

"I have a job offer," Tiff exclaimed as soon as they were seated at the Top View. "It's for a maternity wear company. They want to build an ad campaign using a woman as she goes through the stages of pregnancy. Is it perfect, or what?"

"It is absolutely perfect," Katie agreed, ignoring the stab of envy that she hadn't landed a job herself. "Did you take care of all your other business today?"

"Yes. I ordered death certificates and sent the two

copies I already had to the insurance company and to Mr. Morley. Phil's body will be sent to the same mortuary in Phoenix where his father's body is. I'm trying to think of something I can do to commemorate both of them. The woman I dealt with at Morton's Funeral Home is going to help me figure out what to do."

Katie shook her head. She should learn to stop underestimating Tiff's ability to handle things.

"So, what time do you want to move into our house?" Tiff continued.

"Not before ten o'clock," Katie said.

Tiff laughed. "Well, that's no problem for me, but you usually start your day earlier than I do."

Katie took a deep breath. "Tiff, I have arranged for a police officer to sweep the place for bugs before we move in."

Tiff visibly deflated. "Why would you need to do that?" she asked.

Marta had come up to the table and overheard Katie. "Yes, why would you need to do that?" she repeated.

"Because we don't know Fred Boyson," Katie said. "And, at this point, we can't afford to take any chances."

"I know Fred," Marta said. "I brought you together. You can't honestly believe he has anything to do with the problems you have been having."

Katie squirmed and looked to Robert for support. He looked as helpless as she felt. "We don't know anything," she said. "But it seems too coincidental that he offered us exactly what we needed exactly when we needed it. Anyway, if there are no bugs, we can probably eliminate him as a suspect. That would be good, wouldn't it?"

Marta glared at Katie through narrowed eyes. "I expect a huge apology tomorrow after no bugs are found in the house," she said.

"You'll get it," Katie promised. "I hope, for your sake, that none are found."

A double shot of bourbon hardly dulled Katie's anxiety. Even with Robert watching her, it took a huge strength of will to stop there.

"How about pizza tonight?" she asked, not letting herself suggest what she would have preferred: that they stay right there, where she could get another shot of bourbon along with a hamburger.

"I don't feel like pizza," Tiff pouted.

"Why don't we go to the ZigZag and have a real dinner?" Robert suggested. "A problem that I need to handle has come up at work, so I made a reservation for an afternoon flight tomorrow. Unless something happens to Nana between now and then, it's back to work for me."

Katie could hardly believe how much Robert's words stung. This was her meddlesome older brother, after all. "Even if we find something troubling at the new place?" she asked.

"Your law enforcement, such as it is, will have to deal with that," Robert said. "I came here to see about Nana—and she seems to be settled for the next couple of weeks at least. I can come back later if you need help with her situation. There's nothing I can do about the rest of your problems."

Katie wished he had a more protective instinct. But, hadn't she spent most of her life claiming she didn't need his help?

The three of them had a quiet dinner at the café. Katie glanced across at Tiff. She seemed to be lost in thought. Was she worried about how precarious her future was? She had taken on at least half the rent for Fred's house and a part-time job that would only give her a few hours of work in the next nine months. She might well wonder if she would be free to worry about even that much.

They went their separate ways after eating. Katie returned for what was probably the last night in Nana's house. She was surprised at how empty it felt. She gathered up her belongings so she could make a quick start in the morning.

Pouring herself a nightcap, she went outside and wandered the few steps possible in each direction around the house. She knew, when she put her mind to it, she could think of a good use for the house. Right now, she had too many other things to think about.

Despite everything, she fell asleep almost immediately when her head hit the pillow.

Friday morning, wind rattling the windows and whistling through the trees awakened her. Showering and dressing quickly, she went outside and raised her arms to take it in. The wind's cleansing power seemed to pick up her tension and carry it away.

She loaded up her car. It was too early to go to the new rental house, so she drove to the motel and caught Robert as he was leaving.

"Join me?" he asked. "I was going to do Wendy's, but we can go to the café if you prefer."

"Wendy's is fine," she said. "That'll be faster, and I imagine you want to get on the road pretty quickly."

"Yes, I need to get to the airport, and I want to stop and see Nana for a few minutes first." He studied her for a moment. "You know, I'll be worried about you. And so will Mom. You be sure to keep us informed about what is going on, both with Nana and with you."

"I will," she promised. "Now, I want you to spend the rest of our time together telling me more about your Olivia and the two boys Mom and Pete are adopting."

They spent the next half hour doing exactly that. Hugging Robert good-bye, she wondered if she had made the right decision moving so far away.

When Katie arrived at the house a few minutes before nine, Officer Wilson was already there, going around the perimeter with a meter of some kind.

"Nothing out here," he said when she stepped out of the car. "Of course, I don't know what good any devices out here would do."

"Thank you for checking, Officer Wilson. I wouldn't have thought about that. I'm relieved. Maybe we won't find anything inside either."

"Ken, please. Now, you stay out here. If there are listening devices, I don't want whoever put them there to hear us talking about looking for them. If there are cameras, they'll know soon enough."

Cameras? Katie shuffled from one foot to the other, wanting to peek in the windows to see if Ken was finding anything. When he finally emerged, she realized how much she was hoping she was wrong and he would have good news.

She wasn't. He didn't.

CHAPTER TWENTY-ONE

Ken called Chief Browning to inform him he had found listening devices in the house. The chief showed up a few minutes later with another officer. "Get every fingerprint in that house," he commanded. The officer scurried off and Ken followed.

Chief Browning turned on Katie. "You sure did bring a truckload of trouble to my town."

"I didn't bring it," Katie objected. "I landed in the middle of it—and I don't like it any better than you do."

"Well, looks like that idiot is involved after all. He goofed up this time. Planting those things in the house he is renting to you—is he nuts or something?"

Katie shook her head. Indeed, what was Fred thinking? If he did it. She scrunched her eyes shut. With all the coincidences involving Fred and the house, it was easy to think he was involved. As much as she might want to keep thinking he was, this no longer made sense. Whoever was behind everything that had happened appeared to be expert at distancing themselves from any chance of blame. If it was Fred, why would he meet them in person and rent them a house where he had planted evidence that would implicate him in the crimes?

She would bet that the only fingerprints in the house belonged to people who were known to have been in it. The person who planted the devices would be too smart to leave any trace behind. Who else had access to the house? Or did someone break in?

"Uh, Chief Browning," she said, reluctant to rile him any further. "Could you have the doors and windows checked for signs of forced entry?"

Sticking his thumbs in his belt, Chief Browning rocked back on his heels and studied her through narrowed eyes. "So, now you changed your mind about this guy? You think someone broke into the house and planted those things? How would they even know you were going to rent it?"

"Obviously someone has been keeping track of everything Tiff and I do. They may have overheard us talking at my grandmother's house. It's easy to think Fred rented the house to us to keep an eye on us, but, if so, he must have known the chances of the devices being found were great; and, of course, we did find them."

"Well, give me a clue," the police chief said, a sneer on his lips. He held up one hand and counted off on his fingers with the other. "Tiffany Wells is not guilty.

Jeffrey Crane has ironclad alibis for both murders. Now you say it isn't this guy Fred Boyson, either. So, when are you going to do my job for me and find the real murderer?"

Kate felt a heartbeat of hope in his pronouncement. "You don't seem to be harassing Tiff anymore and we haven't heard from the Phoenix police for a while. Have you both given up your wild-goose chase?"

"Don't you believe it. You probably just let the only other suspect off the hook. She has a couple of high-priced shysters who are muddying the waters, but we'll get her. You can bet on it."

"Who besides Fred do you suppose would plant all these tracking and listening devices and manufacture evidence against her?"

"Why, you, of course, to throw us off the track. And when we catch you at it, you'll go to jail along with her."

He turned on his heel and strode away as Ken and the other officer emerged from the house.

"I guess we're done here," Ken said. "I heard you ask, but there is no sign of forced entry. If I were you, I'd have the locks changed."

"Good idea. Thank you, Ken," she said. "Our land-lady might not like it, but she and Fred are now the only viable suspects, so I don't much care."

Tiff arrived shortly after Ken left, taking her belongings to the larger bedroom. It took Katie a heartbeat to realize their positions had been reversed, since the house was leased to Tiff.

Katie filled Tiff in on what they had found in the house as she unloaded her own belongings. She was about to tell Tiff she wasn't going anywhere before the locks were changed when the locksmith drove up.

"Every lock in the house needs to be changed," she told him. "And please, also check to make sure all the windows can be securely fastened."

"Do you need a security system?" he asked.

Katie hesitated. She hoped this was a temporary place for them to stay, so she didn't want to put too much money into it.

She looked at Tiff. "I think we can wait on that for now. What do you think, Tiff?"

Tiff nodded. "I think whoever did this will know we are on to him and be afraid to try anything here again."

That small explosion at the other rental crossed Katie's mind. She hoped she was correct in thinking they wouldn't try the same thing twice.

"What is on your schedule today?" Katie asked Tiff when the locksmith was gone.

"Not much. I have to do a 'before' photo shoot for the maternity clothes magazine tomorrow."

"Do you have to go to Prescott for that?" Katie asked, remembering the last trip they had made. She couldn't let Tiff drive there by herself.

"No. The photographers will come here. They like the idea of staging it in a smaller city. And I can't do much of anything else until I can send out more death certificates and get stuff put in my name. Phil's life insurance company informed me they would not disburse any funds until the charges against me have been cleared up."

"Have you actually been charged in either case?"

"No. Mr. Leighton said both courts decided there wasn't enough evidence to charge me at this time. Both police departments said they would continue looking for the evidence they needed to get me charged. Even though I don't think he suspects me anymore, Jeffrey is insisting that the inheritance we both get be put into trust until everything is cleared up, and Mr. Morley says I shouldn't fight it as long as I can get some income from it until that happens. Jeffrey agreed to that."

"Has Mr. Morley found out anything more about the Build Them Up Foundation?"

"Nothing. He is taking steps to keep them from being able to claim any of the estate until they can prove they are what they represented themselves to be to Dad."

"I hope that works. In the meantime, we need to spend today getting settled in. I'm for hitting the thrift shops for furnishings, if it's all right with you. I also need to get the food out of Nana's house and decide what I can borrow until, and if, she returns to it. If we do a grocery shopping, we should be set for the time being."

They shopped until almost noon, when Katie left Tiff at Nana's house to rest while she ran over to the clinic to see Nana.

When she arrived, she found Nana using a walker to creep down the hall, followed by a physical therapist who held a belt around her waist. It hurt to see how unstable she was when only a few days earlier she had been walking normally. But it was amazing to see her back on her feet.

"How is my house?" Nana asked as soon as the therapist left. She eyed Katie with suspicion.

Katie grinned. "Your house is fine. I've cleared out the food so nothing spoils while you're away and no pests will get in. May I also borrow a few things for my new place?"

"Borrow only?"

"Yes. When you return home or when I can afford more of my own furnishings, I'll return them."

"I know you don't want me to go home." Nana's lower jaw jutted out.

"I promise you that house will still be there when you can return to it. In the meantime, I was thinking we might find some commercial use for it." At Nana's startled look, she hurried on, "A small boutique or offices that can easily be removed to make it your home again when you are ready."

Nana was shaking her head. "Don't want to be away that long. You can stay there."

Katie shook her head. "No, Nana. Your house is too small for me to live in. I really don't know how you do it." What if she needs a walker, Katie thought. She won't be able to move. "I won't change anything now, but I want you to think about it."

Nana shook her head again. "Don't need to. It is my house."

"You're right," Katie said, a knot in her stomach. If they did need to do something about the house, it would mean a fight with Nana. She wondered on which side Mrs. Andrews, or the court, would come down. She banished the thought. It didn't matter. She couldn't fight with her Nana over it. They would keep it as long as she was alive and wanted to keep it; even if she could never move back into it.

Katie stayed a little longer, trying to ease Nana's mind, but it felt as if a trust had been broken and they might never be able to regain it. Before she left, the nurse informed her Dr. Pelson had left orders for Nana to be moved to the Rest Easy Nursing Home the next day.

———————————

Katie picked up Tiff at Nana's house. They stopped at the ZigZag Café for a late lunch. She asked their server where they could rent a truck to pick up the furniture that had been put aside for them at the thrift shops. Greg came out of the back room.

"How is it you are on the late shift but you are working days every time I need to see you?" Katie asked.

"Karma," he replied with a straight face. "I filled in this morning for a friend, and I'm finished now. I have a pickup and would be glad to help you move your furniture."

"Thank you. I really appreciate it," Katie said. "So, how did your exams go?"

"Aced 'em." He broke into a grin. "Now I'm free until next term."

Katie and Tiff finished their lunch and led Greg to the places where they had purchased furniture. Katie borrowed the twin bed and a bedside table from Nana's house; and Tiff splurged on a new, queen-sized mattress set and frame. By five that afternoon they had a sparsely furnished home and were ready for a break.

"The Top View before getting groceries," Katie pronounced. "May I treat you to a drink for all of your help, Greg?"

"I can't stay long, but I'll join you for a beer before heading home. I have an early shift tomorrow."

"I'll drive," Tiff said. She grinned at Katie. "Mother Hen won't let me drink."

As soon as they were seated, Marta hurried up to their table with their usual drinks. "So, how many listening devices did you find?" she demanded. Her belligerent look told Katie she hadn't heard about the multiple discoveries.

"I'm sorry," Katie said. "We did find a few. But I don't think Fred was the one who planted them."

Marta was deflated. "So, why is he suddenly invisible?" she asked. "I have a feeling I'll never hear from him again." She set down the drinks and marched away.

Katie figured Marta was well out of whatever game Fred was playing, especially if he was still married. It looked as if he had used Marta to get to Tiff and her. But why would he do that if he wasn't involved with the murders and threats?

She looked at her watch. "I guess the chief wouldn't be too happy if we bothered him again today, but I hope he is planning to bring Fred in for questioning." She frowned. "I can't help but think Fred deliberately sought us out to rent the house. While it doesn't make sense for him to do that if he planted the devices, he had some reason for his actions."

She stopped, realizing she was prattling on, and took a good swig of her drink, nearly choking. She forgot she hadn't added any water yet.

"Why are you so anxious to make Freddie look guilty of something?" Tiff asked, her voice querulous. "He seems like a great guy to me."

"I'm not trying to do anything to Fred," Katie said. "I'm trying to get to the truth so we can go on with our lives."

When they left the bar, Katie nearly fell asleep on the short ride back to the house. They had decided against grocery shopping.

A movement caught her attention. She sat up quickly. "Stop!" she hissed at Tiff, but their lights had already alerted the trespasser. He bolted from the front door, which he seemed to be trying to unlock. "Call 911," Katie instructed and jumped out of the car to race after him.

The intruder ran around the side of the house. The person's size and the way he moved convinced her not only that it was the same person who had been trying to break into her rental to plant stolen goods from Mr. Wells' house, but that it most likely was a woman.

This time the person had not been breaking in. Whoever it was had a key and was trying to unlock the door.

Katie raced after the intruder, managing to keep the figure in sight as they ran through brush and across another side yard out to a street. The intruder fumbled at the door of a familiar white sedan, allowing Katie to close in and catch the first part of the license plate number before the car sped away. "BKY" she muttered as she stopped and put her hands on her knees, catching her breath.

By the time Katie got back to the house, two police officers were there.

"I don't see any signs of attempted forced entry," said an officer Katie had not seen before.

"That's because he had a key," she said.

"If he had a key, why didn't he get in?"

"Because we had the locks changed today. You can ask Chief Browning about that, and also inform him of this incident. I got a partial plate number. It begins with the letters BKY."

"Well, I guess we're done here," the officer said. "Anything you want to add?"

"A drive-by once in a while might be nice. But I don't really expect another attempt tonight."

Katie and Tiff calmed themselves with activity, setting up their beds, bedside tables, and dressers. When they ran out of steam, Katie poured herself a drink and put together a peanut butter sandwich.

Tiff flopped down on the sofa Greg had helped them place in the common room, looking wan. "You'd better get a good rest tonight," Katie said. "You want to look good for your photo-shoot tomorrow."

Tiff grinned. "Thank God makeup can hide a lot."

Katie went to her room deep in thought. Fred had to be connected somehow. Otherwise, how did the bugs get in the house and where did their intruder get a key? She was tired of spinning her wheels, waiting for the other shoe to drop.

CHAPTER TWENTY-TWO

At six thirty the next morning, Katie's cell phone jarred her from a sound sleep. "Are you available for work today?" a wide-awake voice chirped.

Katie struggled to clear her mind. "Uh, yes, I guess so," she managed. When her thinking clicked into gear, she frowned. "On a Saturday?" she asked.

"Yes. A small company right there in Cactus City needs someone to handle the phones and do a little typing. They currently have a big project that is time sensitive, so they need to work all of this weekend to get it done." The cheery voice made it sound as if Katie had won first prize.

Maybe she had. A surge of excitement brought her out of bed. "Perfect." It wasn't hard to match the caller's cheerfulness now. She grabbed a notepad and pencil from the bedside table. "I'm ready for the details."

She felt a little deflated when she hung up. Ten fifty an hour wasn't going to help her much. Did all temporary jobs pay so little? Looking at her notes, she frowned again. The agency had given her an address, a phone number, and a person to report to. What was the name of the company? Oh, well, that might have been an oversight.

Forty-five minutes later, Katie was showered and dressed. Not knowing how her day would go, she managed a bowl of Cheerios while throwing together a sandwich for lunch.

She knocked on Tiff's bedroom door as she left. "I have to go. I got a job," she called. She would have to phone later to be sure Tiff knew where she was.

The address took Katie to a nondescript one-story residential house with no identification on the exterior. The door was locked. After a moment's hesitation, she rang the doorbell. A slender young man with owl-like glasses, who appeared to be a teenager, unlocked the door and showed her to a desk in what must once have been a small living room.

"Name's Jimmy," he said. "Welcome aboard." He disappeared into a back room.

Okay. Names are good. A person to report to and what she was supposed to do might help too. She looked around. A few computer books sat on a book-shelf. She didn't see a file cabinet. Whatever they did must not involve a lot of paper, unlike the corporate law environment she was accustomed to. A small kitchen was off to one side, with a sink, refrigerator, microwave, and a coffee maker. Putting her sandwich in the refrigerator and investigating the cabinets, she found the makings for a pot of coffee and put one on to brew. Before returning to her desk she explored the rest of the room to determine which door led to the bathroom.

Back at the desk she familiarized herself with the drawers. The file drawer contained a few financial forms and correspondence along with copy paper and envelopes. She tried to check out the computer, only to discover it was password protected. She glanced at the door Jimmy had disappeared through but decided if she was supposed to get into the computer files, he would have given her the password. By the time the next person came through the door, a woman close to her own age, she was beginning to wonder what she was getting into.

"What a welcome smell," the woman said, heading straight to the coffee and placing a box of pastries beside it. "It looks as if you found your way around quickly."

"As far as I could," Katie said, standing.

The woman came over with her mug of coffee and shook Katie's hand.

"Loretta Swanson," she said. "I head up this group. I'm sorry I wasn't here when you arrived, but thank you for coming in at a moment's notice. Our receptionist had a family emergency, and we're not sure how long she'll be out."

"Kate Christensen. The kid in the back room let me in, and," she hesitated, "I guess I'm available as long as you need me, but I have no idea what you do or what I'm supposed to do."

Loretta laughed. "First things first. We deal in a

lot of confidential information here. I got caught off-guard when Maxine called last night to say she would be out today, so I took a risk having you come in before talking to you." She put a form in front of Katie. "Please read this over. It is a promise not to discuss work-related issues outside the office. If you are comfortable with that, sign the sheet and we're good to go."

Katie read it over. The name at the top of the form was Confidential Research, and it was a pretty standard confidentiality agreement. She hesitated about signing it only because she knew nothing about the company.

"I don't suppose anything you do is illegal?" she asked.

Loretta smiled. "I have to admit, you might catch Jimmy doing a little hacking. That's the 'kid' in the back room." Her eyes twinkled, and Loretta's stress on the word "kid" made Katie wonder how old Jimmy really was. Loretta went on, "Mostly we do online research on companies and people."

"Oh!" Katie took a breath, grabbed a pen, and signed the paper. She hoped she wasn't jumping into something she would regret, but she might get a little online research opportunity, and that was too good to pass up. Besides, she wasn't committing herself to anything except not talking about the company.

Loretta handed Katie a time sheet and showed her how to fill it out.

"Now, even though the position is receptionist, we don't get any walk-ins and very few phone calls. Most of our business comes through our company e-mail, which you distribute to the staff. You can forward it all to me until you learn what kinds of things each person handles. Our main business is information searches for private investigators and commercial institutions, with a few individual clients thrown in. Keeping a low profile helps us maintain the necessary confidentiality. You won't have a lot to do, even though we are kept busy in the back rooms. What you do frees us up to concentrate on that work, and you are a buffer for us should we need one."

Loretta sat at the desk and wrote on a sticky note. "This is the password for getting into the computer," she said. "Memorize it and tear it up." She typed it in and clicked on a folder where the staff sent the results of their research. She showed Katie another folder that contained several forms Katie would use to transform the information into a report. After a few more instructions, Loretta joined Jimmy while Katie began to fill out the first form with information that had been compiled yesterday. Two other staffers eventually ambled into the office, grabbed donuts and coffee, introduced themselves, chatted a minute, and proceeded to the second of the two rooms in the back. Evidently promptness was not a virtue for this group.

Katie refilled the coffee pot and went back to work. It wasn't long before everything in her work file was done. She forwarded a couple e-mails to Loretta, noting that they were both for background checks.

She was itching to try a little research herself, but

decided she had better clear it with the boss. She dialed Loretta's number. "Are there other things I should be doing now?"

"No. If Maxine doesn't come back soon, I'll start you on a little filing and keeping financial records up to date, but for now you can fill your time however you like," Loretta said.

Katie blinked. Filing? There were about three pieces of paper in the office. Then she realized Loretta meant organizing on the computer.

"Would it be all right for me to do some research of my own?"

"That's perfectly fine," Loretta said. "It may prove useful to have someone at the front desk with that capability."

Katie knew Mr. Morley had searched some specific sites, like charity databases, for the Build Them Up Foundation. Not knowing exactly where he looked, she started with her own search on the foundation's name. Her first search resulted in sites with instructions for building house foundations and for giving children solid foundations, but not what she was looking for. Eliminating the word "foundation" gave her sites for building people up or for body building. Maybe adding words would help. Charity Build Them Up Foundation took her back to foundations but not the one she wanted. She sat back and tried to think it through. How about lawsuits? Had they done this before? And if so, had they been caught at it?

A frustrating amount of searching finally brought

her to a site called rippingyouoff.com. Opening it, she clicked on a tab for scams and blinked. There were hundreds of entries, evidently in order of the date they were posted, with no way she could find to sort them. Looking through a few, she found everything from useless rants to claims of what could well be actual scams. Was it worth going through all of them? It felt like looking for a needle in a haystack. Yet, since it could make such a difference in figuring out what was going on and she had no other avenue to do that, she had to give it a shot.

Before she could start investigating them, two more e-mails came in. After forwarding them to Loretta, three of the staff forwarded information for her to enter into the report forms and e-mail to clients. She was surprised to note the time on the computer screen. Where had the day gone? Immersed in her own research, she had totally missed lunch. This late flurry of activity was probably a normal end of the work day.

"It looks as if Maxine's emergency situation will take at least another day," Loretta said when she came out of the back room. "I hope you're available tomorrow."

"Yes," Katie said. "I look forward to it. This is a perfect fit for me right now."

Loretta nodded. "It must be hard for a person with your qualifications to settle for what you can get in temporary work. Makes me wonder why you do. I'd like to get together with you and talk about it."

So, Loretta had done some checking on Katie's

background. "I'd like that, too, but I can't make it happen today. I haven't talked to my grandmother and she needs to know I'm here for her. Plus, there are some other things going on in my life right now."

A cloud passed over Loretta's eyes. "Well, I hope they won't keep you from being able to complete your duties here."

"I won't let them," Katie said, hoping she could make the statement true. After all, Maxine would be back on the job in a day or two, wouldn't she?

Katie found her way to the Rest Easy Nursing Home to see how Nana had settled in before going home. "I have a temporary job," she told her. "I like it a lot, but I don't know how long it will last."

"Good," Nana said. "Your house?"

"It is very nice," she said. "I'll take you to see it as soon as we can arrange it. I borrowed your bed and bedside table. The rest of the furniture we found at secondhand stores."

Katie was delighted to see Nana manage a slight grin. "Not like your Seattle apartment," she said.

Katie laughed. "No. I've come down in the world. But I like it all the same."

Nana laid back, appearing to be tired out from their short conversation. Katie went out to check with the nurse about her condition.

"She had a lot of physical therapy today," the nurse

said. "She is so determined to get well, we have to be careful not to let her overdo it."

Sounds a little like me, Katie thought. Bull-headed. That must be where it came from.

After a quick stop to pick up a few groceries, she returned to the house to find Tiff collapsed on the sofa.

"Are you all right?" she asked.

"Just tired," Tiff said. "I forgot how much work I had to do to get a few good shots."

"Did you have lunch?" Katie asked.

Tiff grinned. "Yes, mother hen. The crew made sure I kept my strength up as long as they needed me."

"So, is that it for now?"

"Yes, for the maternity set. I'll have to get a little bigger before they do any more of those. The agency plans to use my hands for some jewelry ads, but that won't happen for a week or so, and I'll probably have to go to Prescott to do them."

"I really don't think you should drive to Prescott on your own," Katie said. "At least not until everything is cleared up."

"Maybe you could go with me?"

"If I'm not working." Katie couldn't believe how much she hoped the job she was on would last for a long time. Or how much she resented what felt like Tiff's assumption she would always be there to help her.

"I wonder if Freddie will be at the Top View tonight," Tiff said, her expression wistful.

Katie stared at her. "You surely don't plan on going out now," she said.

"We've been going there every night."

"That's because we had no place else to be," Katie said. "We have our own place now, and I have to get up for work tomorrow. I thought you were worn out."

Tiff pulled a pouty face. "I'm never too tired to go out," she said. "I'd like to go and see if Freddie is there. But, since I can't drink, I guess I'll, like, stay home."

The way Tiff said it made it sound as if it was Katie's fault she couldn't drink, or at least that she couldn't go out. What was this about Freddie anyway?

"Do what you want," Katie said, heading for the kitchen to pour herself a bourbon. "I'm going to eat this sandwich I made for my lunch, make a phone call or two, and go to bed early."

Katie was relieved when Tiff huffed off into her room. She wasn't feeling sociable, but didn't want to feel as if she was neglecting her. She hadn't had a roommate since law school. She had forgotten how stressful it could be.

The phone calls never got made. As soon as Katie had eaten, finished her drink, and brushed her teeth, she fell asleep.

———

On her way to work the next morning, Katie stopped to pick up some finger food for lunch. Once the work she was being paid to do was finished, she would resume her own search and not want to take the time to eat a real meal.

The office was locked when she arrived, so she rang the doorbell. Jimmy opened the door a moment later, gave her a grin, and disappeared. Did the guy never go home? She started the coffee, used the chart Loretta had shown her before leaving yesterday to forward e-mails that had come in overnight to the appropriate staff person, and filled out a couple of reports as Loretta and the others trickled in the same as yesterday.

By mid-morning she had completed her work and returned to the rippingyouoff.com website. It took too long to find where she had left off, but once there she found she could race through most of the listings, knowing by their titles they had nothing to do with her search. When one of the staff members sent her work, she shrank her window and opened a new one to do it, returning to the website as soon as she could.

In the middle of the afternoon, she found something that sounded so close to the Build Them Up Foundation she thought it must be related. It was a rant from a man whose elderly father had been convinced to leave his life savings to an organization that said it provided scholarships for needy students. It was called the Help Them Out Foundation, and the representative had the necessary paperwork to prove the claim. Even though the family had no choice but to hand the money over after the father died, they had never been able to find any trace of the organization. Printing out the information, she decided to keep looking for more.

"Are you up for another day of work tomorrow?" Loretta asked when she emerged from the back room.

"Oh, yes," Katie said. She pointed to the computer screen. "Is there any way I can keep this window open so I don't lose my location?"

"Yes, we can do that," Loretta said. She walked over to Katie's computer and hit a few keystrokes. "Done. May I ask what you're looking for?"

Katie considered for a moment. She had cut Loretta short yesterday. Maybe she could make up for it today. She could probably use Loretta's help.

"It's kind of a long story," she said. "Do you have time for a drink today?"

"Top View Bar?" Loretta asked.

Katie grinned. "How did you know?

"To tell you the truth, I've seen you in there. But it's the best watering hole in town. I'll see you in about fifteen minutes."

When Katie walked into the bar, she stopped in her tracks. Tiff was there, sitting with Fred Boyson. Marta, a stormy look on her face, slammed drinks down in front of them. Tiff jumped back as the liquid slopped over the rim of her glass.

Loretta arrived, and Katie started to lead her to a table away from Tiff's, but Fred looked up and saw her.

"Katie," he said, waving her over. "I had an appointment in Cactus and dropped by to see how things were going at the house. Tiff suggested we come here and have a drink."

"You went to the house?" Katie asked, alarmed.

"Yes. Tiff showed me how nicely you have decorated it on so little."

Katie frowned at Tiff before shifting her gaze to the drink in front of her. Tiff took a sip and let out a squeal. "Marta, I did ask for a virgin, didn't I?"

"Not that I heard," Marta spat out, grabbing the glass and heading back to the bar.

"Join us," Fred invited.

Katie shifted her glare to him. She wanted desperately to ask him about his wife, but she didn't want to let him know she had been checking up on him. "Marta wondered what had become of you," she managed.

He had the good grace to look uncomfortable. "I got busy with a few things," he said.

"Maybe we can talk another time," she said. "I need some time alone with my boss right now."

Katie led Loretta to a table across the room from Tiff and Fred.

Loretta looked at Katie. "A lot going on there that I don't know about," she said with a laugh.

"There sure is." Marta arrived with Katie's bourbon and a glass of white wine for Loretta. "You must be as regular here as I am. I never noticed."

"Not always at the same time. And you usually seemed too busy to look around much. Now, you were going to tell me what all your research is about."

Katie told her she was researching scams against older people. She suspected one called the Build Them Up Foundation was a scam since she couldn't find any information on it. "If it is, I'm afraid Fred is involved somehow," she said, her voice low. "He seemed to court Marta as a way to get to Tiff and me to rent us the house, which was filled with listening devices when we were ready to move in. I Googled him a couple days ago and discovered he works in insurance and is, or at least was, a married man."

"What have you found so far on that website?" Loretta asked.

"A complaint from a man who lost all his late father's estate to a similar outfit, calling itself the Help Them Out Foundation. Since all the paperwork was in order, there was nothing his family could do about it."

Loretta tapped a fingernail against her wine glass. "So, you think it's the same group as the Build Them Up Foundation?"

"That's about it," Katie said. "But people are being murdered, and I can't help but think there's a connection." She stared at the table where Tiff and Fred were deep in conversation. "Excuse me a minute." She took out her cell phone and dialed the police department. "Is Ken Wilson there?" she asked.

Ken came on the line a moment later. "Ken, is there any way you can get away for a few minutes and meet me at the house? I'd like to have you do another sweep. Oh, great ... thank you."

"I'll talk to you in the morning," Loretta said as they stood to leave. "We'll see if we can dig a little deeper into this."

Katie waved to Tiff, making it look as if she was leaving with Loretta. Once outside, they went their separate ways, and a few minutes later Katie opened the house door to Ken.

Ken did a quick sweep of the house. "Nothing," he said.

"I'm sorry I wasted your time, but thank you for putting my mind at ease," she said.

After Ken left, Katie paced around the house. Why did Fred come, if not to plant more devices? She gave herself a mental slap. Of course, he wouldn't be doing that. It would point the finger directly at him if they were found after the others had been cleaned out. But that still left the question—why was he really here?

CHAPTER TWENTY-THREE

Katie heard Fred and Tiff return at about ten o'clock. Katie stayed in her room, door closed. That's what roommates did, whether they approved of what was going on or not. She heard Fred decline Tiff's offer of a nightcap, saying he had an early appointment in Phoenix tomorrow.

As soon as he left, before Katie could talk some sense into herself, she stormed out and confronted Tiff. "What were you thinking?" she asked. "That man may be involved with the threats against you. And you let him into the house? You're lucky he didn't plant more of those listening devices."

Tiff looked at her through slightly unfocused eyes. Katie knew she was acting like a mother hen but she couldn't stop herself. "Tiff, you know you shouldn't be drinking."

"I didn't drink that much," Tiff said, though her condition indicated otherwise. "Besides, I can decide for myself what I should or shouldn't be doing. And if Marta can't hang on to a man, that's her problem."

"Of course," Katie said. "Forget I said anything. It's on your head." She stomped into her room and slammed the door.

Okay, now who was acting like an adolescent?

———————————

It felt good to return to the calm of her work environment the next morning. Katie already felt at home there, even while wondering if this type of work could keep her challenged for long. She hoped whatever was wrong in Maxine's life would keep her away for a while longer so Katie would have time to finish her own research.

"I've given some thought to your problem," Loretta said when she came in. "I'm sure you plan to keep looking for more instances of this scam. But in the meantime, I'll also get Jimmy to try to track down these foundations."

"I can't afford ..." Katie started.

Loretta cut her off. "No argument. It's one of the perks of working here."

Between bouts of doing the work she was being paid to do, Katie continued through the seemingly endless list of rants about real or perceived wrongdoings. It wasn't until she was about ready to wind it up for the day and go home that she found another one.

When Loretta came out of the back room, Katie

showed her a copy of the complaint. "This one is called 'Give Them a Boost.' It looks like the same thing."

Loretta looked at it. "I'll put Jimmy on this one, too. He's having fun trying to get through to these guys. If he can't, it probably isn't worth your time to try and find more. They'd cover their tracks the same way." She handed the copy back to Katie. "But I have bad news for you. Maxine is returning to work Tuesday." She gave Katie her business card. "We are going to keep working on this, because what these people are doing isn't right and that's what this company is all about. I want you to stay in touch. And, if Maxine's family problems take her away again, I hope you'll consider coming back to us."

"I'd like that. Also, I'm going to forward these two cases to Mr. Morley, the attorney for Jim Wells, who I believe was scammed by this Build Them Up Foundation."

"You can do that before you leave," Loretta said. "I'd love to join you for a drink again tonight, but I have another engagement."

"I need to spend some time with my grandmother, anyway. I can't believe I didn't even talk with her yesterday."

"I doubt she'd want you to put your life on hold in order to watch after her, especially when she is being well cared for," Loretta said.

Katie thought about that after she e-mailed the information to Mr. Morley and was on her way to see Nana. She did want to spend time with Nana, but she knew she'd have to maintain balance in her life or resentment could build up.

Katie took a closer look today as she approached the Rest Easy Nursing Home. It was housed in an adobe building with rounded corners nestled in a flat area landscaped with various-sized stones and prickly pear cacti. The inside of the building was decorated in muted greens and roses, giving it a warm, comfortable feel.

Katie entered Nana's private room, noting that it, also, was decorated in soothing tones. "I want to go home," Nana declared. Katie turned around and went back to the front desk.

The nurse there smiled and shook her head. "She is making progress, but it'll be a while before the doctor wants her to go home, unless she has full-time care."

"If I could talk her into a bigger house, we might be able to manage that," Katie said. "Do you think she will be able to live independently again?"

"You'd have to ask the doctor, but my guess would be no, not completely. She might not need full-time care, but she'll probably need some care and monitoring."

Katie returned to Nana. "Not yet, Nana. You know, you moved into that house after Nano died because you didn't need a big place anymore. Now, it appears that you do. If you lived in a larger house, still your home, we could have someone stay with you as long as you needed it."

"I don't need someone," Nana insisted.

Katie was impressed that she was talking in

complete sentences. It raised her hope that she truly could live in her own place again. But, if Nana even needed to use a walker, Katie could see no way she could navigate that tiny house without some major remodeling. How was she going to convince Nana?

Katie's phone rang before she left the facility.

"Ms. Christensen, this is Paul Morley. I received your very interesting documents and we'll be following up on them. I wanted to let you know I've contacted the Build Them Up Foundation and told the person I spoke with that someone from the foundation needs to come to my office and sign some papers in order to complete a transfer of the funds. She asked if it would be all right to come in tomorrow."

"I want to be there," Katie said. "I don't know if the person will be someone I've seen before, but I'd like to know all the players in whatever game they are playing."

"Where have you been?" Tiff asked when Katie arrived at their house. "I've been so alone all day."

"No Freddie?" Katie asked before she could stop herself.

Tiff's lower lip shot out like a two-year-old about to have a tantrum. "What is the big deal about my seeing Freddie?" she asked.

"You know that Marta thought he was interested in her. And now he's interested in you? I don't think so."

She went to her room and returned with the copy she had made of Fred Boyson's wedding announcement pulled up on her laptop. "He used Marta to get to us, and now he's using you for some reason. He was, and might still be, a married man, Tiff."

Tiff stared at the picture for a moment before retreating into her bedroom, slamming the door behind her.

Katie sighed. I have no one to blame but myself, she thought. I let myself be dragged into this mess, and I have to find my way out. She didn't bother to tell Tiff where she was going tomorrow or ask if she wanted to go, even though the trip was to protect Tiff.

CHAPTER TWENTY-FOUR

Katie was on the road by eight the next morning. She made sure her GPS recognized the rental address as her home address for the return trip in case she got turned around in Phoenix. It was only an hour and a half drive, but she wanted to meet Mr. Morley and have some time with him before the Build Them Up Foundation representative arrived.

She also hoped to get her first look at the majestic views between Cactus City and Phoenix and find out how far down the mountain she would go before the saguaro cactus appeared. Unfortunately, once she was on I-17, trucks materialized in front of her whenever she came around one of the many curves, and cars whizzed past her if she stayed anywhere near the posted speed limit; so she had little opportunity to enjoy the scenery. The heavy traffic, once she hit the valley approaching Phoenix, felt enough like I-5 through Seattle for her to relax a bit.

It was almost ten o'clock before she found a parking lot three blocks from Mr. Morley's office. That was close enough to walk and far enough to distance herself from her bright-red, very identifiable Maserati. As soon as she exited the car and started toward the office building, she realized she had the wrong clothes on. Nothing she could do about it now. She would have to learn to layer if she was going to live in Arizona.

She entered the lobby of the towering building where Mr. Morley had his offices and stopped. People scurrying toward the elevators were a painful reminder of the constant pressure in the life she had left behind. With a deep breath, she took careful, measured steps to the security desk where, to her surprise, she had to sign in. The guard pointed her across the lobby to the elevator bank that rose to the 22nd floor. Mr. Morley, whose law firm appeared to take up the whole floor, met her at the elevator.

"You knew I was here?" she asked.

"The guard calls from the lobby when you sign in," he said. He led her to his suite and motioned to an ivory wingback chair behind a Queen Anne coffee table before turning to a tray with coffee and fixings on the credenza behind him.

"Cream, sugar?" he asked.

"Black is fine," Katie said, looking around. As a low-level attorney at her firm, not yet making partner, her office hadn't had anything like the cushioned forest-green carpeting, plush furniture, and floral drapery that Mr. Morley enjoyed.

Once they were settled with their coffee, Mr. Morley showed Katie the addendum to the trust in which Jim Wells left the residue of his estate, after the bequests to Tiffany, Jeffrey, and Lila, to the Build Them Up Foundation. It was signed, witnessed, and appeared ironclad.

Comparing it with what she had found from the rants on the website, Mr. Morley agreed they all appeared to be the work of the same group.

"I've alerted the fraud investigators," Mr. Morley said. "They might not have paid attention to one complaint, but when we have three with similar patterns they are sure to take notice, especially since this last one evidently involves murder. Good work finding those other two."

Katie shrugged off the praise. It was not brilliance, but doggedness, that had led to her discovery. "Of course, the problem is finding out who they are," she said. "I hope this person you will meet with today will help us do that. At least we will get a look at one of them. They can't use a messenger service to sign official papers. Did they have to put their address on the papers Mr. Wells signed?"

"Yes, but it doesn't do us any good. I thought I'd give them a visit, but the address led us to an empty lot. Now, I don't want them to know you are here," he went on. "That might put you in jeopardy for your trip back to Cactus City. You'll need to be out of sight when the person comes in."

Katie thought for a moment. "When the person

leaves, I think I should follow to see if I can discover their location. The problem is, they would spot a bright-red Maserati, especially if they were the ones who planted the tracking devices on it. They'd definitely know it was me."

Mr. Morley shook his head. "No. It's much too dangerous for you to try to follow them. I've called a private investigator I work with to do that."

"But he won't be able to recognize anyone, and I might. We need to get this figured out before someone else gets hurt. I believe these people are going to keep trying to make Tiff miscarry. If they can do that, and make sure she is convicted of the two murders, plus add Jeffrey to her list of victims, they'd stand to double their take."

Mr. Morley hesitated another moment. "I suppose you could ride along with the investigator," he ventured. "But, he will be taking pictures so you don't have to be there to identify the players."

"What if people go in different directions after they meet?" Katie asked. "If they don't, I can leave it to the investigator, but if they do? Besides, they might decide to bolt. That would leave Tiff the only suspect in the murders."

Mr. Morley studied Katie for a long time. Finally, he opened a desk drawer and pulled out a set of keys. He held them out, but pulled back when she reached for them. "I'm only doing this because I already have private investigators on the scene. More than one, so they can follow in different directions if needed. You might spot something neither of them would recognize as significant, but it'll complicate things if they have to look after you too. If I loan you a car, you need to promise not to do anything foolish. Losing money is one thing. Risking your life is a totally different matter."

"I promise," Katie said. She hoped she would have no reason to do anything dangerous, but two lives had already been lost and, as far as she could see, more were at risk. Delaying action might give these people time to hide half of Mr. Wells' estate, where it could never be retrieved.

"The car is a blue Ford Taurus in slot number seven on the first floor of the parking garage." He handed her a round, blue token along with the keys. "This will get you out of the garage free and quickly. I'll give the person who comes to sign the papers a red token, which isn't normally used for that purpose. I'll let the garage attendant know to let that car out and signal you and the private investigator, who will be outside the building. Don't get out of the car at any time. Once you've discovered if you can identify anyone, call it in and return here. My men will handle it from there. Are we clear?"

"Clear," Katie said, fidgeting a little. She'd have to wait and see what she needed to do when the time came.

A few minutes before eleven, Katie positioned herself in another doorway in the hall outside Mr. Morley's office, where she could see who entered without being seen herself. She pressed her lips together to suppress a gasp of surprise when a woman she didn't recognize stepped off the elevator. Katie had expected a woman, but not this one. While this woman was just as slender, she was several inches taller than the one Katie had spotted in Cactus City.

As soon as the woman was in Mr. Morley's office and the door closed, Katie took the elevator to the garage, found the Ford, and positioned it where the attendant could see her.

Not more than ten minutes later, the attendant signaled that the red token had been used. The woman had wasted no time signing the documents. A familiar white sedan exited the garage. Katie waited a beat before following. As she did, a nondescript gray Chevy pulled away from the curb in front of the building and followed the white sedan. Katie stayed two car lengths behind the Chevy, even when adrenaline pushed her to get closer. She had to trust that the private investigator knew what he was doing.

The sedan avoided the 101 loop and Route 51, staying on city streets, making numerous turns, which Katie thought must be a tactic intended to lose any possible tail. When the Chevy turned right while the sedan kept going straight, Katie followed the sedan, figuring the detective was making an evasive maneuver of his own. Sure enough, two blocks later the Chevy appeared behind her.

Finally, the sedan pulled into a no-parking area in front of a small office building. The woman jumped out and hurried into the building. Katie, heart beating with anticipation, double parked in the next block where she could keep an eye on the doorway through her rearview mirror. She called Mr. Morley to give him their location, even though she was sure the detective had already done it. Her call would show him she was following directions.

A few minutes later, the woman came out with a companion. Katie sat up straight and turned to get a better look to make sure she wasn't mistaken about who it was. Even though she was no longer wearing the hoodie or hat, this woman was undoubtedly the person who had been causing so much havoc in Cactus City. She even still sported the bandage on the wrist where Katie had hit her with a rock. But now, Katie could see her clearly enough to recognize her from Fred Boyson's wedding picture. It was his wife. She called Mr. Morley to let him know.

When the two got in the white sedan and drove off, Katie expected the private detective to follow, but instead he got out of his car and went into the building. She peered around, growing nervous. Where was the other detective? Obviously, someone had to get whatever information was in the building, but someone also had to follow the sedan.

Katie pulled out and fell in a few cars behind it. The driver's continued evasive maneuvers had Katie totally disoriented by the time she had driven through several residential streets and parked in the driveway of a neat bungalow. Katie drove on, past a few houses, before parking and calling in the address to Mr. Morley. She gripped the phone when another car pulled in right behind her. Was someone else involved?

"What are you doing?" Katie jumped when Mr. Morley's voice boomed in her ear from the phone. "You should have come back to the office after getting the first address and identifying the woman."

"Your private investigator stayed there. Someone had to follow the sedan to its next location."

"My private investigator's partner did that," Mr. Morley said.

Katie felt a little foolish when she looked in her rearview mirror at the car behind her. "In a dark-blue Dodge?" she asked.

"Yes," Mr. Morley said. "Your job is done. You need to come back here now."

"Can you find out who owns this house?" Katie asked.

"We already did. When you told us Fred Boyson's wife was involved, we looked up his address. That is where you are now. And that office building where you stopped houses the insurance company for which Mr. Boyson works."

Oh, no. Katie had almost convinced herself he wasn't involved, even though she now knew his wife was.

"We are connecting the dots and have given all the information we have to the police," Mr. Morley said. "There is nothing more you can do. I'm calling in the private investigators so we don't do anything to muddy the waters, and I expect you to come too."

"I don't think we should do that," Katie said. "What

if they get suspicious and make a run for it? What if they have another car in the garage that we wouldn't be able to identify?"

"It's a police matter now. We need to leave it alone," Mr. Morley insisted before disconnecting.

A moment later, the car behind Katie pulled out and disappeared down the street. Katie's stomach tightened when she realized she was now alone, with no idea where she was or how to get back to Mr. Morley's office. She had left her GPS in the Maserati.

Closing her eyes, she took a few deep breaths. No problem. She could figure out how to use the one on her phone when the time came. She looked in her rearview mirror at Fred Boyson's house. For now, she would stay right here and keep an eye on the house until the police arrived.

Half an hour later, there was still no sign of the police. Had Mr. Morley not made a strong enough case to convince them to come? Hands beginning to shake, Katie called Mr. Morley again.

"I believe they have decided they need to look into this themselves before they make any moves," he said. "But, I repeat, it is in their hands now. You need to get back here before I report that car you are in as stolen."

He wouldn't do that, Katie thought. "I'll wait here a little so I can follow them if they decide to go somewhere else," she said, disconnecting quickly and biting her lower lip. How long could she sit here before attracting attention—or needing to use a bathroom? She stared at her shaking hands. Did she have any idea what she was doing?

When she raised her head to look around, she shrank back against the seat. Someone was standing so close to the window on the passenger side of the car that all she could see was a torso. Her chest constricted. She grabbed the driver's door handle. Before she could open the door, another torso appeared there. That person had a gun. Katie hit the door lock.

The gun tapped against the window, a totally unnecessary gesture to get her attention. Katie cracked the window a tiny bit and looked up. Fred's wife, Alana, she remembered from the wedding announcement, stepped back far enough for Katie to see her face.

"Get out of the car," she said quietly. "I think you'd better come with us."

CHAPTER TWENTY-FIVE

Katie froze, her eyes desperately searching the neatly tended adobe houses up and down the street. No cars, no people. She was tempted to stay where she was. These women murdered two people and managed to put all the suspicion on Tiff. They wouldn't do something right here in the open that they couldn't blame on Tiff. Would they?

But her eyes were riveted on the gun waving in her face. Was there anyone around to hear a gunshot? Katie swallowed over a lump in her throat, thinking fast. Alana and the other woman must realize they'd been discovered. They might decide to just shoot her and get out of town.

She waited a good thirty seconds before, unable to think of some action that would help her, she got out of the car. The women gripped her arms and pushed her along. The flat, stony yard, with its artfully arranged cactus offered no obstacle she could use to throw them off and try to escape.

Too soon, they were inside the house, the door shut behind them. Katie looked around a modern, cream-and-white living room, searching for some way to defend herself. How stupid was this? She should have stayed in the car, open to view. Now she was at their mercy.

Could she get her hands on one of those brass figurines to use as a club?

Taking a deep breath and straightening her shoulders, Katie decided she wasn't giving up yet. She needed to talk, to stall them, while she figured out what she could do.

"Hello, Mrs. Boyson. How is your wrist?" Katie was surprised that her voice didn't reflect the quaking inside her.

Alana looked startled. "How ...?" She shook her head. "What are you doing here?" she hissed.

"I'm searching for the people who are trying to frame Tiffany Wells for murder and cheat Jim Wells' heirs. You seem to be likely suspects." Katie eyed the kitchen. It would have knives and skillets and other possible weapons, but how could she get over there?

"Who is she, Alana?" the taller woman asked as she pulled Katie farther into the room, closer to a coffee table with a large, heavy-looking ashtray on it. Could she reach it before Alana pulled the trigger?

"Kate Christensen. Tiffany Wells' friend." Alana turned back to Katie. "Why would you expect to find anyone here who would do such a thing?"

Katie blinked. Did Alana really believe they hadn't been exposed? Evidently not, because a moment later she added, "What are we going to do with this meddler, Lila?"

Lila. Jim Wells' wife. Jeffrey was correct when he said she was a gold digger. The two women must have known each other before Lila married Jim Wells, since they had apparently run the scam at least two other times.

Lila stared at Katie for a moment. "I don't know. But I do know we need to cut our losses and get out of here."

The door burst open and Fred charged into the room. He stopped and stared from one woman to the other. "What's going on?" His voice shook. "What have you two involved me in?"

Katie's mind whirred again. Fred was not surprised to find Lila and Alana together. He knew they were acquainted. He sounded alarmed about what they were doing, but that could be an act. Was he involved?

Alana turned on Fred. "Oh, don't be such a wimp. Do you have any idea how much money we're talking about?"

"I make good money," he said. "You've never wanted for anything."

"Only a villa in France and a private jet and a few other niceties I could mention. Your 'good money' doesn't compare to what we could do with six or seven million dollars on top of what we already have."

"What you already have?" Fred asked, his voice growing weak.

"I think she's alluding to what they got when they

called themselves the Help Them Out Foundation," Katie said. Maybe he really didn't know what they'd been up to. "Or maybe the Give Them a Boost Foundation. It's not the first time they've pulled this scam. And they might have succeeded again if they hadn't become greedy once they discovered how large Mr. Wells' estate is."

"You can't prove anything," Lila declared, but her face had lost its confident sneer.

"So, what are we going to do with her?" Alana asked again.

Lila stared at Katie for a moment. "We can't get rid of her here, and we don't have time to set something up. It looks like it's time for us to disappear. The only question is how."

Katie nearly sank to the floor with relief. Maybe she could get out of this alive. "Right. If you shot me, you'd have no way to blame it on Tiffany," Katie said.

Hoping to keep the women occupied until the police arrived, if the police were even coming, Katie turned to Fred. "Why did you let Marta think you were interested in her? Was it simply to get Tiff and me to rent the house, so you could listen to our conversations on the listening devices you planted?"

Fred frowned, a look of confusion on his face. "Listening devices? I don't know anything about any listening devices." He threw an accusing glance at Alana. "Alana convinced me it would be doing you and Tiff a favor, as well as her friend Taylor, if you rented the house from Taylor."

Katie heard a faint sound of sirens in the distance. They seemed to be drawing nearer. *Turn them off*, she thought.

Alana lifted her head and looked at Lila with alarm. "We have to get out of here now!"

"You idiot," Lila spat. "If you hadn't been so greedy we could have walked away with at least three million."

"Too late to worry about that," Alana said, grabbing Katie by the wrist and pulling her through the kitchen to the garage door. "We still have the other money. Let's go."

"No, Alana!" Fred grabbed the arm Alana was holding Katie with. "You're not going anywhere with Katie."

Alana's hand lost its grip as she continued toward the door. "All right, you take her. Come on Lila, let's go."

Alana trained the gun on Katie and Fred as she backed through the kitchen to the garage, hitting the garage door opener. Lila raced past her and jumped into the driver's seat of a dark-gray Mercedes Benz. She had the car moving before Alana made it into the passenger seat. As soon as she did, Lila stomped on the gas. Katie ran to the garage door, hoping the police would arrive before they could make their escape.

They were out of the garage and almost even with the white sedan before Lila turned her head around to look behind her. Too late. With a loud crunch, the Mercedes backed into Fred's car which was parked directly behind them in the driveway.

As two Phoenix police cars pulled up in front of the

house, the two women jumped out of the Mercedes and ran back into the garage. Lila had time to hit the garage door opener, closing it. Katie jumped back and grabbed a knife from the kitchen counter, but the gun was again aimed at her before either she or Fred could react. The knife clattered onto the tile countertop.

"Well, I guess it's good we didn't kill you," Alana said, her voice cool as she prodded them back to the living room. "It appears we'll need you as a bargaining chip."

"You can let her go," Fred said. "I can be your bargaining chip."

Lila laughed. "Who is going to believe you are an innocent bystander?" she asked. "They were all your insurance customers and you rented ..."

Alana raised her hand, cutting Lila off. "Don't say anything more," she said. "It could be used against us."

Lila laughed again. "Alana, dear sister, no one is going to use anything against us. Either they will both be dead, or we will be. I'm not in favor of going to prison."

Sister?

Alana didn't look as if she agreed. For a moment, the gun wavered. Lila grabbed it from her.

"So," Katie said, surprised at the calm that settled over her. She looked from one woman to the other. "The police are outside. You have no means of transportation. What do you plan to do?"

"I plan to walk you out of here and get in your car. As long as we have you, they won't dare approach us," Lila said.

Katie jumped when a loudspeaker blared outside. "Come out with your hands up and no one needs to get hurt."

"Ha." Alana appeared to have her resolve back. She opened the door a crack. "We're going to walk out of here and drive to the airport or two people in here will get hurt."

The police tried negotiating, but Alana held firm for safe passage to the airport and a flight to Ecuador. If the police backed off, she said they would leave Fred here and take Katie with them. As soon as they landed in Ecuador, they would leave Katie on the plane and go on their way.

Katie didn't want to risk her life on the hope that the two women could be trusted. She didn't want to get on any airplane going anywhere with them. She thought of her mother's crime-solving talent and silently begged for guidance. But she didn't think her mother had ever found herself in a situation like this. Probably because she was never stupid enough to put herself in a situation like this.

The police looked as if they thought Alana had given them a workable solution. Katie could only hope they had another scenario in mind and weren't actually planning to make this one happen.

With guns trained on them from behind the squad cars, Alana and Lila pushed Katie and Fred out of the house. They started in the direction where Katie had parked her car and stopped short. It wasn't there.

"Where's the car?" Alana demanded.

"We're bringing one for you now," an officer said.

"No, I want the car she came in," Alana said.

"What car?" asked the officer.

Katie frowned. Mr. Morley's car was not where she had parked it. Her eye caught a movement at the corner of the house next door. Her eyes widened when she recognized Jeffrey. What was he doing here?

Alana frowned, seemed to consider the missing car for a moment. "So, where's the car you are getting for us?" she asked. She started to pull Katie back toward the house only to discover two policemen had circled around behind them.

While the women were distracted, Katie watched Jeffrey step away from the corner and fling something toward them. A knife sliced through the air and pierced Lila's gun arm. With a scream, she dropped the gun, which slid onto the stony yard. Fred jumped away from Lila while Katie and Alana both dove for the gun.

Alana reached the gun first. Katie knocked it out of her hand. It skittered across the stones into the street. A policeman grabbed it. The police started to close in, but stopped when Alana pulled the knife from Lila's arm and held it to Katie's throat. Lila screamed and grabbed her arm, now gushing with blood.

"Get our car and let us go or I'll kill her," Alana shouted. Jeffrey stood back, holding another knife. He hesitated, looking around as if searching for a target. Katie had a moment of regret that she had ever suspected him, but it quickly passed as the blade of the knife Alana held pressed harder. If she moved, it would dig in.

A car pulled up beside the squad cars in front of the house and a police officer in SWAT gear got out. "Give the keys to Lila," Alana demanded.

"They're in the car," the officer said, backing away from it.

Katie steeled herself. She had no intention of getting into any car with this maniac. The knife eased up slightly as Alana started to push her forward. The policemen moved slowly, surrounding them as they moved away from the house. It's now or never, Katie thought, and dug in her heels. The knife blade pressed against her throat, drawing blood. Ignoring the pain, Katie raised a foot and stomped hard, landing on Alana's instep. Alana cried out. The blade sliced across and off of Katie's neck. Katie whirled and shoved Alana as hard as she could. Alana stumbled, tried to right herself, but two policemen grabbed her before she could regain her footing.

Katie had time to see that the police had grabbed both Fred and Lila before hands clutched her arm. She twisted around, ready to strike out again. Jeffrey let go, backing up. "Whoa," he said. "It's me. They've got the bad guys. And you need a doctor."

Katie turned to see the police handcuffing Alana and Lila. Fred was already in the police car. A moment later an officer with a medical bag arrived.

"I'm the SWAT medic. An ambulance is on its way," he said, looking at Katie's neck. "This cut isn't too deep, but it'll bleed a lot," he added, instructing Jeffrey to put pressure on the wound while he went to bandage Lila's arm.

Jeffrey grinned. "You'll probably need stitches. They'll be your badge of courage."

"I didn't feel very courageous," Katie said, her voice weak. "Desperate is more like it. But you—do you always go around carrying knives?"

"Well, I don't own any guns, and I have experience with knives. Remember I told you I participate in knife-throwing competitions? I always keep two knives in the trunk of my car for when I might have a chance to get in some target practice. When Mr. Morley called to tell me what you were up to and I realized the kind of danger you were putting yourself in, I had to do something. What were you thinking?"

"I only wanted to get this over with so we could all go on with our lives. But you are the last person I expected to come to my rescue."

"I told you I wasn't the bad guy you thought I was."

"Did you steal Mr. Morley's car?"

Jeffrey grinned. "You know, you shouldn't leave the keys in the ignition. Mr. Morley told me what kind of car he loaned you. When I saw that mess in the driveway, I thought those two might try to use his car. I moved it around the block before you came out of the house."

Katie managed a weak smile and was surprised to discover the EMTs had to pry her hand from Jeffrey's when they put her in the ambulance.

CHAPTER TWENTY-SIX

Katie withstood stitches by the emergency room doctor, a scolding from Mr. Morley for not following instructions, and questioning by the police before she escaped from the emergency room three hours later. The late-afternoon heat felt good when Jeffrey, who for some reason was still at her side, escorted her out of the austere building.

"Thank you for all you've done, Jeffrey." Katie wondered why he bothered to help someone who had so recently accused him of murder. "Now, I'll take a cab to retrieve Mr. Morley's car." She wasn't sure if she could walk the few blocks from the office building to her own car, but she'd worry about that later. "I think I'm going to find someplace to spend the night. I'm not up to the drive back to Cactus City."

"Mr. Morley already had his car picked up," Jeffrey said. She frowned at the shiver she felt when he placed his hand on her arm, guiding her through the parking lot. "My car is right over here, so I can take you to yours." He gave her a sideways glance. "If you'll trust me to drive that hot Maserati, I'll take you all the way to Cactus."

The eagerness in his tone made her think he might be more interested in driving the Maserati than in helping her get back home.

"So, you can be stranded there?" she asked.

"Not really. There's a shuttle from Cactus City to the Phoenix airport, and plenty of public transportation from there. Anyway, after our rocky start, I'd like to get the chance to know you better."

Katie decided to take him up on his offer. She had questions for him too. They were silent for most of the drive from the hospital to the parking lot where she had left her Maserati. Katie studied the street names on the route they took, hoping a little of it would stick in her memory. While she didn't plan to ever live in the hot desert valley where Phoenix was located, she expected she would have to learn how to find her way around the city.

"How did you turn up at Fred's house at precisely the right time?" she asked after they had switched cars and Jeffrey steered the Maserati onto I-17.

"When Mr. Morley realized you weren't returning to the office, he sent one of the PIs back to make sure you were safe. The PI got there in time to see those two march you into the house. He informed Mr. Morley, who called Fred and me and the police and everyone else he could think of to try to get you out of the trouble you insisted on getting yourself into."

Katie bristled, but only for a moment, before deciding Mr. Morley was a very smart man, and she was a very lucky woman. "Did you really think Phil only came to see his father in order to protect his inheritance?"

Jeffrey nodded. "I did. I still do. He never had time for his father until Uncle Jim married that woman."

Katie was silent for a moment. She hoped she never got so busy with her own life that she didn't stay in touch with her mother. That was easy when she lived close by, but might be more difficult from this distance. "Tiff seemed to care about Mr. Wells."

"Tiffany is an actress as well as a model," Jeffrey said, frowning. "Uncle Jim was her ticket to the good life. She probably hoped he would take care of her when she told him she was pregnant."

"That might have happened if Mr. Wells hadn't been murdered," Katie said. "She has plenty of money now, but my guess is she still needs someone to take care of her."

A huge yawn overtook Katie. It had been a long, tiring day, but she planned to enjoy the views going back up the mountain since it was a rare opportunity to do so while someone else was driving. She put her head back and closed her eyes to rest them for a moment.

Katie sat up and blinked. They were already driving into Cactus City. "I can't believe I fell asleep," she said. "I'm sorry I was such bad company. I need to go to the nursing home and check on my grandmother before doing anything else. Shall I drop you off at the shuttle depot first?"

"No, I'm in no hurry," Jeffrey said. "Let's do what you need to do and get something to eat before I leave. I'll stretch my legs while you talk to your grandmother."

The cool mountain air swept away Katie's lingering sleepiness. She felt a smile spread across her face as it sank in that the murder investigation was over. Her mood lifted even more when she found her grandmother sitting up in her cheery room, awake, alert, and stronger than seemed possible in such a short time.

"Oh, my dear, what happened to you?" Nana cried when Katie walked in.

"I'm fine," Katie said, fingering the bandage on her neck. "I'll tell you all about it later. But those problems with Tiff are behind us now."

The understanding in Nana's eyes heartened Katie. It was apparent she remembered what had been going on, and seemed relieved that it was no longer a problem.

"So, you can take me home?"

Katie raised her eyes and prayed for guidance from the God her mother had convinced her would help her figure things out. "That's up to your doctor," she said. "I'll talk to him as soon as possible and see what he says."

After talking with Nana for a few more minutes, Katie leaned in to plant a kiss on her forehead. "I have to leave now, but I'll be back for a longer visit tomorrow."

She stopped by the nurse's station on her way out to see if the doctor had left any instructions.

"Yes. He has a meeting in Phoenix tomorrow, but he left instructions to move your grandmother to assisted living where she can continue rehab. He thinks she'll need to be there at least two weeks before he's comfortable letting her go home."

One problem solved, another one to handle, Katie thought. "Do you know what time of day she'll be moved?"

"Only that it'll be sometime in the morning. Do you want us to inform you when it happens?"

"No, I'll just need to have the location so I can visit in the afternoon."

The nurse handed Katie a map with directions.

Katie returned to Nana's room to let her know what she had learned, then walked out of the building in a bit of a daze. The good news was the doctor expected Nana to be well enough to go home. The question was whether she would be able to live in that house.

Katie took a deep breath, her mind already sorting through possibilities. A shower instead of a tub for sure. Maybe open up the living areas into a great room. Nana certainly didn't need a full kitchen any more. Take out the dividing wall between the bedrooms.

Find out if an addition could be managed, for some-one to stay with her.

How much could she change the house and have it still feel like home to Nana? She'd have to remem-ber to get Nana's permission for any changes, or Nana might not be happy with them. Could Katie get anything done before the doctor said Nana could go home? If there was any way to make it possible, Katie would take Nana home to what felt like her own house when she was released from assisted living. She hoped she could figure out the logistics of that move before the time came to do it. She was quite sure it wasn't a permanent solution, but maybe Nana could see for herself that it wasn't working before the next move had to be made.

She got back in the Maserati and Jeffrey drove to the house she shared with Tiff. No light was vis-ible when they arrived. "My guess is Tiff is at the Top View," Katie said. "But I'm surprised she would go there by herself. Shall we go see, or eat at the café?"

"Let's see if that's where she is. I think she and I need to make peace with each other."

"Don't you have to get back to Phoenix tonight?" Katie asked.

"I'll go tomorrow."

Katie mulled that over while they proceeded up the hill to the Top View. "Let me get this right. You drove me home so I didn't have to stay at a motel, and now you have to stay at a motel?" she asked when they left the car and approached the bar.

He grinned at her. "How else would I manage all

that time alone with a beautiful green-eyed girl like you?"

Katie was sure it was the warmth of the bar that made her flush when Jeffrey opened the door. A familiar roar from the sports fans in the back room cheered her. She stopped in the doorway for a moment, feeling strangely at home. She looked around the softly lit room, more like a cozy café than a bar.

She caught sight of Tiff and Fred at a table in the middle of the room. What was Fred doing here? She had expected the police to arrest him along with his wife and sister-in-law. Instead, he and Tiff appeared to be celebrating.

Katie led Jeffrey to the table. "Katie," Tiff gushed. "My hero." She jumped up and threw her arms around Katie. "Thank you, thank you."

Katie extricated herself from Tiff's grasp and readjusted the bandage on her neck. "Well, you're welcome for whatever I did, but I didn't do it alone, and what I did do was rather foolish." Reluctantly, because she still didn't like the man, she added, "Fred tried to convince those two women not to hurt me, but, Jeffrey deserves most of the thanks. He saved my life."

Tiffany frowned as she looked at Jeffrey. "Freddie didn't tell me that. But thank you." She turned to Fred, beaming now. "And, thank you, too, for keeping her safe."

Not quite what I said, Katie thought. Marta approached with a double bourbon and a glass of water and placed them on the table. Katie followed her back to the bar when Marta went to get the beer Jeffrey asked for. "I know it feels as if you were cheated and dumped," she said, "but I guarantee you are better off without Fred in your life. There will be someone much better for you in your future."

Marta gave her a wan smile. "Thank you. I guess I figured that out, but it still hurts. It seemed like such a good thing for a while there." She looked over at the celebration. "Tiff seems to have taken to him."

Katie's gaze followed hers. "Unfortunately, it seems she has. But, I have a feeling they might be better suited to each other." She stepped back over to join the table, and Jeffrey stood to pull out a chair for her.

Katie savored the first sip of her drink. It was so much more pleasant than the painkillers she would have to do without after drinking it. "Except for the itching that has already started under this bandage, I'm feeling better already." She turned to Jeffrey. "I'm sorry we got off to such a rocky start."

"Mostly my fault," Jeffrey said. "It seemed to me that Tiff was the only one who could have done it. I didn't look deeper, under the surface, the way you did."

Tiff's tinkling laughter came across the table. "How much is that now? Almost three million apiece after taxes?"

Jeffrey frowned. "How do you figure that? The trust gives us each a million and a half, period."

"What do you mean? With everyone else out of the way, we must each get half. And after what those two women put us through, I think we deserve it, don't you?"

"I don't think either of us deserves any, but you aren't paying attention. Uncle Jim left us a million and a half each. That is all we are entitled to. Neither that fake foundation nor Lila will be able to get anything Uncle Jim left to them because they murdered Uncle Jim for it, but I don't know how the courts are going to decide what to do with it. It would be nice if they could find a trustworthy education fund to put it in, which is what he wanted."

Katie agreed that would be nice, but she also wondered if there was any way Phil's unborn baby could get some of it. If the court did decide to award anything to the baby, Katie hoped they would set up a legal guardianship for the child that didn't give Tiff control.

"Hey," Fred said, his eyes slightly glassy. He had obviously been celebrating a lot for a man whose wife had been arrested for murder and fraud. Or maybe he was drowning his sorrows. "Take whatever you can get."

"And what's your interest in this?" Jeffrey asked, giving Fred a sharp look. "I can't believe you didn't have a hand in it, especially since Mr. Morley tells me all the people who were ripped off were clients of yours. I'm surprised the police let you go."

Fred had the decency to look uncomfortable. "Well, they want to talk with me some more. But, I knew nothing about it. Alana and her sister used me to find marks. When they came across Jim Wells, they evidently decided Lila should marry him and they would try for all of his estate." He relaxed. "Now, I'm just happy for Tiff," he said, wrapping an arm over her shoulders. He looked at Jeffrey. "What are you going to do with your share?"

Jeffrey was silent for a moment, as if in thought. Then he said, "I have a good job and a solid savings plan. I'll probably add to that savings plan, but I recently got my broker's license, so I might open my own real estate firm." He glanced at Katie out of the corner of his eye. "Possibly in Prescott or Prescott Valley, maybe even Cactus City, if it continues to grow as fast as it has been the last couple years."

Katie squirmed. Was he hinting at some kind of future for them?

Tiff practically bounced with excitement. "Well, I want my own modeling agency and school. I think there is too much competition in Phoenix. Prescott is an almost untapped market, but I'll check other places, too, like Flagstaff and Sedona." She beamed a coy look at Fred. "Will you help me, Freddie?"

"I could do that," he said. He flashed his wide smile. "I haven't looked into my options yet. It's pretty certain I won't be able to work as an insurance agent after word gets out that I was clueless about my wife stealing from my clients."

"So," Katie turned to Fred, "what is going to happen to the house?"

"That's in limbo," Fred said. "It belongs to Alana,

but I didn't know that. She hired a woman to act as owner so I wouldn't know what she was doing. Between the divorce I'm going to get and the legal actions against her, I don't know how long it'll be tied up. In the meantime, unless someone in authority tells you differently, you might as well stay there."

"Tiff?" Katie asked. "Are you staying there for a while or moving to Prescott right away?"

"As soon as the money comes through and I figure out where I want to go, I'm moving," Tiff said. "I'm sorry to leave you, Katie, but the lease is month-to-month so you can take it over if you want to."

Katie shook her head. Tiff certainly wasn't going to put much effort into helping Katie in repayment for the support she had given her through all of this. In fact, now that Tiff's situation had been resolved, Katie wasn't sure she wanted to spend more time with her. "No, I want out," she said. "The explosion at the vacation rental wasn't my fault, and there is no longer any risk of a repeat. I'm sure the landlord will have to let me back in for the six weeks left on my contract."

Katie hoped that was true, and she was pretty sure when she put her mind to it the landlord could be convinced it was in his best interests to let her finish the lease. She wanted to put this whole episode behind her and start fresh. At least, as fresh as it could be, given Nana's situation.

Katie turned to Jeffrey. "My grandfather wanted the remainder of his estate after my grandmother is taken care of to go to a scholarship fund. I don't know how much will be left when she is gone, and I hope she lives for a long time, but I plan to do a lot of research, starting right now, so we don't get caught in some kind of scam like Mr. Wells did."

Jeffrey's eyes narrowed in thought. "If whoever has control of the rest of Uncle Jim's estate decides to honor his wishes, maybe we can research it together. They might listen to a recommendation from me."

Katie felt herself draw back. It sounded as if Jeffrey wanted to see more of her; however, one of the issues she still hadn't dealt with was the rejection she'd experienced in Seattle. Maybe another relationship so soon wasn't a good idea.

Yet, she couldn't help but think that she didn't need to put absolutely everything about this episode behind her.

ACKNOWLEDGMENTS

This book would probably never have been completed without the input of the accomplished writers in my writer's critique group: Judith March Davis (*Pagoda Dreamer*), Mary Ann Clark (*The Baron's Box*), Edward Gates (*A Ranger's Time*), Dougal Reeves (*Trees*), and William Johnstone (*The Seventh Message*).

Hints and corrections from the Prescott Police Department helped me believe I might actually have most of it right. Any errors remaining are purely my fault.

And, of course, I couldn't get the book finished and published without the invaluable work of my editor and book designer, Mary Jo Zazueta.

ABOUT THE AUTHOR

Patrica K. Batta (Pat) grew up in Northern Michigan. She attended Northwestern Michigan Community College, received her BA from the University of Puerto Rico, and a Master's in Teaching from Oberlin College in Ohio.

She married and moved to Philadelphia, and later to Seattle, Washington, where the Marge Christensen Mystery Series was born. She moved back to West Chester, Pennsylvania, and then returned to Michigan before settling in Prescott, Arizona, where she has begun the Katie in Cactus Mystery series.

Contact Pat at facebook.com/patriciabatta and see more about her work at lillimarpublishing.com.

Made in the USA
Columbia, SC
02 December 2017